Erle Stanley Gardner and The Murder Room

››› This title is part of The Murder Room, our series dedicated to making available out-of-print or hard-to-find titles by classic crime writers.

Crime fiction has always held up a mirror to society. The Victorians were fascinated by sensational murder and the emerging science of detection; now we are obsessed with the forensic detail of violent death. And no other genre has so captivated and enthralled readers.

Vast troves of classic crime writing have for a long time been unavailable to all but the most dedicated frequenters of second-hand bookshops. The advent of digital publishing means that we are now able to bring you the backlists of a huge range of titles by classic and contemporary crime writers, some of which have been out of print for decades.

From the genteel amateur private eyes of the Golden Age and the femmes fatales of pulp fiction, to the morally ambiguous hard-boiled detectives of mid twentieth-century America and their descendants who walk our twenty-first century streets, The Murder Room has it all. ›››

The Murder Room

Where Criminal Minds Meet

themurderroom.com

T0345453

Erle Stanley Gardner (1889–1970)

Born in Malden, Massachusetts, Erle Stanley Gardner left school in 1909 and attended Valparaiso University School of Law in Indiana for just one month before he was suspended for focusing more on his hobby of boxing that his academic studies. Soon after, he settled in California, where he taught himself the law and passed the state bar exam in 1911. The practise of law never held much interest for him, however, apart from as it pertained to trial strategy, and in his spare time he began to write for the pulp magazines that gave Dashiell Hammett and Raymond Chandler their start. Not long after the publication of his first novel, *The Case of the Velvet Claws*, featuring Perry Mason, he gave up his legal practice to write full time. He had one daughter, Grace, with his first wife, Natalie, from whom he later separated. In 1968 Gardner married his long-term secretary, Agnes Jean Bethell, whom he professed to be the real 'Della Street', Perry Mason's sole (although unacknowledged) love interest. He was one of the most successful authors of all time and at the time of his death, in Temecula, California in 1970, is said to have had 135 million copies of his books in print in America alone.

By Erle Stanley Gardner
(titles below include only those published in the Murder Room)

Perry Mason series

The Case of the Sulky Girl (1933)
The Case of the Baited Hook (1940)
The Case of the Borrowed Brunette (1946)
The Case of the Lonely Heiress (1948)
The Case of the Negligent Nymph (1950)
The Case of the Moth-Eaten Mink (1952)
The Case of the Glamorous Ghost (1955)
The Case of the Terrified Typist (1956)
The Case of the Gilded Lily (1956)
The Case of the Lucky Loser (1957)
The Case of the Long-Legged Models (1958)
The Case of the Deadly Toy (1959)
The Case of the Singing Skirt (1959)
The Case of the Duplicate Daughter (1960)
The Case of the Blonde Bonanza (1962)

Cool and Lam series

The Bigger They Come (1939)
Turn on the Heat (1940)
Gold Comes in Bricks (1940)
Spill the Jackpot (1941)
Double or Quits (1941)
Owls Don't Blink (1942)
Bats Fly at Dusk (1942)
Cats Prowl at Night (1943)
Crows Can't Count (1946)
Fools Die on Friday (1947)
Bedrooms Have Windows (1949)
Some Women Won't Wait (1953)
Beware the Curves (1956)
You Can Die Laughing (1957)
Some Slips Don't Show (1957)
The Count of Nine (1958)
Pass the Gravy (1959)
Kept Women Can't Quit (1960)
Bachelors Get Lonely (1961)
Shills Can't Count Chips (1961)

Try Anything Once (1962)
Fish or Cut Bait (1963)
Up For Grabs (1964)
Cut Thin to Win (1965)
Widows Wear Weeds (1966)
Traps Need Fresh Bait (1967)

Doug Selby D.A. series

The D.A. Calls it Murder (1937)
The D.A. Holds a Candle (1938)
The D.A. Draws a Circle (1939)
The D.A. Goes to Trial (1940)
The D.A. Cooks a Goose (1942)
The D.A. Calls a Turn (1944)
The D.A. Takes a Chance (1946)
The D.A. Breaks an Egg (1949)

Terry Clane series

Murder Up My Sleeve (1937)
The Case of the Backward Mule (1946)

Gramp Wiggins series

The Case of the Turning Tide (1941)
The Case of the Smoking Chimney (1943)

Two Clues (two novellas) (1947)

Traps Need Fresh Bait

Erle Stanley Gardner

An Orion book

Copyright © The Erle Stanley Gardner Trust 1967

The right of Erle Stanley Gardner to be identified as the author of this work has been asserted in accordance with the Copyright, Designs and Patents Act 1988.

This edition published by
The Orion Publishing Group Ltd
Orion House
5 Upper St Martin's Lane
London WC2H 9EA

An Hachette UK company
A CIP catalogue record for this book is available from the British Library

ISBN 978 1 4719 0926 9

All characters and events in this publication are fictitious and any resemblance to real people, living or dead, is purely coincidental.

No part of this publication may be reproduced, stored in a retrieval system or transmitted in any form or by any means without the prior permission in writing of the publisher, nor be otherwise circulated in any form of binding or cover other than that in which it is published without a similar condition, including this condition, being imposed on the subsequent purchaser.

www.orionbooks.co.uk

CHAPTER ONE

It was about three-thirty in the afternoon – the time when lunch counters begin to fill up with persons playing hooky from the business offices in nearby skyscrapers, persons who are looking for an afternoon coffee break with perhaps a piece of pie a la mode, or a sandwich for those who have weight problems.

Having no weight problem, I was craving sweets and was about to ask Elsie Brand, my secretary, to go out and join me in an ice cream when I saw a peculiar red flickering light on the frosted-glass panel of my private office.

The knob turned.

Someone on the other side kicked the door open, and then I saw what had made the peculiar lights – a circular cake studded with burning candles.

Elsie Brand was in the lead carrying the cake. Directly behind her was big Bertha Cool, the senior partner in our private detective business – a hundred and sixty-five pounds of rough, tough, profane efficiency.

Behind Bertha was the receptionist, and behind her was the stenographer who did the general typing and acted as Bertha Cool's secretary.

As the door swung open, they raised their voices: 'Happy Birthday to you! Happy Birthday to you! Happy Birthday, Dear Donald! Happy Birthday to you!'

Elsie Brand set the cake on my desk, looked at me significantly and said, 'Make a wish and try to blow out all the candles.'

I took a deep lungful of air and blew out all the candles except one.

'You didn't make it,' said Elsie, and her voice was filled with disappointment as if she had been making the wish.

'Fry me for an oyster,' Bertha said; 'the bastard isn't going to get his wish. That'll be the first time.'

The receptionist, a tall romantic gal in her late twenties, laughed musically.

The typist produced a percolator of hot coffee and paper cups. Elsie brought out a knife and said, 'I baked it myself, Donald. It's the kind you like.'

I pulled out the candles, stacked them neatly in an ash tray, and started cutting the cake.

A masculine voice from the doorway said, 'So, *this* is where everyone is!'

We all turned.

The man in the door was trying to be affable. He was a tall, broad-shouldered, slim-waisted individual with a bronzed face. He looked too much like a Texan to be one. There were wind-puckered crow's-feet around his eyes. He had a rather prominent nose and deep calipers running to the corners of his mouth.

Here was a man who could be hard to get along with when he was peeved.

'I seem to have hit the office at the time of a coffee break,' he said. 'Pardon me.'

'A birthday party,' I explained. 'It's my birthday and they're surprising me.'

'Oh,' he said.

Bertha hated to let a nickel slip through her greedy fingers, but she wasn't going to be dominated by any broad-shouldered Texan.

'They come once a year,' she said; and then added, 'Got any objections?'

'None whatever,' the man said. 'My sole comment is that I'd like to be included in the party. I could use a piece of that cake and perhaps talk business at the same time.'

'Well, we haven't got enough chairs in here,' Bertha said. 'It's going to be a stand-up party. How do you want your coffee – black or with cream and sugar?'

'Cream and sugar,' he said.

Bertha looked him over and grunted as she appraised his flat stomach.

Bertha had the figure of a roll of barbed wire, and she alternated between times when she was determined to start taking off weight and times when she said, 'To hell with it. What's the use?'

I cut the cake.

The office party was strangely subdued now that a stranger had intruded.

I gave the uninvited guest the first piece of cake. He gallantly tendered it to Bertha Cool, who latched onto it, picked up a fork from the table and took a big bite.

'Where'd you get the forks, Elsie?' Bertha asked.

'I got the equipment from the restaurant downstairs.'

'Good cake,' Bertha said, then turned to the man. 'What's your name?'

'Barney Adams,' he said. 'I can't produce a card while I'm holding a plate of cake, but after I finish I'll show you that I'm a vice-president in charge of investigations of the Continental Divide Insurance Indemnity Company in New Mexico.'

'What's the idea?' Bertha Cool asked.

'What idea?'

'Having an insurance company in New Mexico?'

'Because it's a fine central location for lots of business,' Adams said. 'We don't cater to the city rich. We want the rural business, and we have quite an outfit at the home office – relatively low land value, lots of room for expansion, unlimited parking space, the advantages of living in a city with a small population – a rural background, if you get it.'

Bertha looked him over again and said, 'I get it.'

Elsie was disappointed, not only because I didn't get my

wish, but because the stranger had butted in on the party – something that had been intended to be an intimate little inter-office gathering.

And anybody could tell from the way Bertha was planting her feet that she was getting ready to talk business.

Bertha took a new forkful of cake, chewed it appreciatively, washed it down with coffee, let her diamond-hard eyes sweep over Adams in another glittering appraisal, and said, 'What's on your mind?'

'Business,' Adams said.

'This is a business office,' Bertha told him.

Adams smiled.

'Except when Donald has a birthday,' Bertha said, 'and the girls get the idea they're going to celebrate. Nobody gives a damn about *my* birthday.'

There was a silence for a minute, then Elsie Brand said, 'No one knows just when it is, Mrs. Cool.'

'You're damn right they don't,' Bertha said shortly.

Adams said, 'I take it that you are Mrs. Bertha Cool, the senior partner of the firm, and that this is Donald Lam, the junior partner?'

'Right,' Bertha said.

'I have looked you up rather extensively,' Adams said.

Bertha merely grunted.

'A rather unlikely combination, if you don't mind my saying so,' Adams went on. 'But you have the reputation of accomplishing remarkable results in cases which have been exceedingly difficult.'

Bertha started to say something, changed her mind and took another mouthful of cake.

'I have a matter of the greatest importance – one which will require very delicate handling and one which is quite unorthodox,' Adams said.

'Uh-huh,' Bertha said in a voice muffled by the cake. 'All our business is like that.'

'I would like to discuss the matter in detail and inquire

into the amount of compensation which you would require to handle the matter.'

Bertha took some coffee and got rid of the mouthful of cake.

'Out that door and into the general reception room,' she said, 'then turn to the right, go down to the door marked "B. Cool, Private", go in and sit down. I'll be in in a minute and we'll talk money.'

'Can't we do it here and now?' Adams asked.

'Hell, no,' Bertha said. 'When I talk money, I want to be sitting in my own chair in my own office.'

'I take it you make the financial arrangements?' Adams asked.

'That's right,' Bertha said, 'either alone or with Donald. Right now, Donald's celebrating, so we can do it alone. I prefer it that way, too.'

Bertha scraped the last of the frosting off her plate, put the plate on my desk, said, 'Nice cake, Elsie,' turned to Adams, and said, 'Come on. Bring your cake and coffee if you want.'

Bertha barged out of the office like a battleship plowing into heavy seas.

Adams hesitated a moment, then put his plate with part of the cake still on it on the desk and tagged along behind.

Elsie Brand said to me, 'Oh, I'm glad they've left! What was your wish, Donald?'

I shook my head. 'Personal and private.'

She said, 'Maybe it will work out all right after all.'

The receptionist said, 'I've got to get back to the telephone.' She walked to the door of the outer office, held the door open and said, 'Coming, Hortense?'

The typist said, 'I was thinking about seconds.'

'Don't,' the receptionist warned. 'Seconds are never as good as firsts.' She held the door open.

The two girls went out. Elsie Brand said, 'Congratulations, Donald!'

'On what?'

'Your birthday, silly!'

I smiled at her. 'And thanks for the cake,' I said.

She came close to me, looked up in my eyes, said, 'Many happy returns,' and kissed me. 'You can make seconds on wishes, Donald,' she said.

'Sounds like a good idea,' I told her.

Elsie, standing close, said, 'I should have asked Bertha to let me lock up the office while we were having the cake.'

I grinned.

'Yes, I know,' she said. 'Bertha and money are inseparable.'

She was still standing close to me. Again she raised her lips to mine. The telephone rang sharply.

Elsie broke away after the second ring, picked up the phone, said, 'Yes?' And the receptionist at the switchboard said in a voice that the instrument made audible for a radius of some feet, 'Bertha wants Donald *right away*.'

'Oh, Donald,' Elsie said, grabbing a cleansing tissue and wiping my mouth. 'Oh, Donald . . . Damn that man Adams anyway.'

I put my arm around her shoulders, drew her to me, held my cheek against hers for a minute, patted her shoulder and went into Bertha's office, leaving it to Elsie to clean up the plates and get the forks back to the restaurant.

Bertha said, 'Sit down, Donald. Mr. Adams says he has quite a story. There's no use having him tell it twice. When he gets through, we'll see if we can handle the case.'

She turned to Adams and said, 'Now, this starts with the ad in the personal columns of the paper?'

'Well, actually,' Adams said, 'It goes back a little before that. We had a similar situation in Portland, Oregon.'

'What were you doing writing policies in Portland, Oregon?' Bertha asked.

He laughed and shook his head. 'The same situation which exists here, Mrs. Cool. The policy was written in New Mexico but the insured traveled by automobile to Oregon and had an accident.'

'This present case has to do with the insurance carrier on a

Cadillac which was involved in the accident referred to in the ad.'

'I see,' Bertha said somewhat noncommittally.

'I don't,' I told him.

Adams took a newspaper clipping from his pocket and handed it to me. 'Read it aloud,' he said. 'The part that's circled with red pencil.'

I read the ad: 'THREE HUNDRED DOLLARS REWARD for information leading to witnesses who can testify Ford Galaxie ignored stop signal at Gilton and Crenshaw and hit gray Cadillac about ten P.M., April 15. Address: Box 685 this office.'

'Three hundred dollars,' I said. 'Some reward!'

'Can't they get witnesses easier than that?' Bertha Cool asked.

'Not the kind of witnesses they want,' I said.

'What do you mean?' Bertha asked.

'Notice the wording,' I said. 'Reward is to be paid only for witnesses who can testify that the Ford Galaxie ignored the stop light and ran into the Cadillac.'

'Well, if that's what happened, what's wrong with it?' Bertha asked.

'Suppose that *isn't* what happened,' I said. 'Suppose it was the other way around. Suppose the Ford had the green light and the Cadillac ran through a stop light. And notice this ad is put in the section for "Help Wanted".'

Bertha blinked her eyes and said, 'Fry me for an oyster!'

Adams said, 'Exactly. This is, in our opinion, an attempt to get witnesses to commit perjury.

'Now heaven knows how widespread this situation is, but, as I mentioned, we ran into a similar situation in Portland, Oregon.'

'I take it,' I said, 'that you're representing the man with the Ford Galaxie, that he's your insured, and naturally you don't want to see him framed so that . . .'

'No,' he interrupted, 'strange as it may seem, we're the insurance carrier on the gray Cadillac.'

'And you don't have any idea who's doing this?'

'No.'

'If three witnesses show up,' I said, 'that would be nine hundred dollars somebody would be paying out. Two witnesses would be six hundred, one witness would be three hundred. Even if there's only one witness, it's a pretty good chunk of dough.'

'Right,' Adams said tersely.

'So if he can't get it out of the insurance company,' I said, 'how would the person who represents this mysterious "Box Six eighty-five" get his money back once he had paid it out?'

Adams shrugged his shoulders.

'What about the case in Portland, Oregon?' I asked.

'That was settled.'

'Did the ad bring in any results?'

'We don't know.'

'And there again the ad was asking for witnesses favorable to you?' I asked.

'No, in that instance the ad asked for witnesses who would be willing to testify on the other side of the case.

'We had some affidavits. Our investigator talked with some witnesses and we decided to settle. It wasn't until afterward that someone dug up an old newspaper containing this want ad and sent it to us, asking if we were interested. By that time, it was too late to do anything.'

'But you might have been influenced in making a settlement because of evidence that had been secured through this ad?'

'Right,' Adams said.

'How much was the settlement?' I asked.

'Twenty-two thousand five hundred.'

'Pickle me for a beet!' Bertha said half under her breath.

Adams said, 'Quite naturally we are concerned about this ad. We want to find out what's back of it. We want to find out who's doing it. We want to find out whether it is a bona fide attempt to get evidence or whether it's an attempt to suborn perjury.'

Bertha said, 'This is in Donald's department. He gets out on the firing line.'

'And the financial arrangements?' Adams asked, and then hurried on. 'Shall we say fifty dollars a day plus expenses?'

'Well, of course,' Bertha said, 'that would represent a fair per diem, and . . .'

'And how much cash retainer?' I asked.

Adams looked at me and grinned. 'I thought Mrs. Cool made the financial arrangements.'

'She does,' I said. 'That doesn't keep me from asking questions.'

'One thousand dollars retainer,' Bertha said shortly.

'Isn't that pretty steep?' Adams asked.

'Not on this kind of a job. If there's any bad faith in connection with it, we're running up against a gang of crooks and Donald will be taking chances.'

Adams looked me over thoughtfully.

'Don't make any mistakes about him,' Bertha said hastily. 'He's no superman with the muscle, but the little bastard has it all upstairs with brains.'

Adams said, 'That's according to the reports I have had. You are considered to be a very efficient combination. However, in order to be fair, I think I should state that my experience in this business is such that I feel the assignment may prove physically dangerous.'

'Donald will squeeze in and out some way,' Bertha said.

'It may be a tight squeeze,' Adams warned.

'What are you trying to do,' Bertha asked, 'run up the price?'

'I thought we had already agreed on price.'

'A thousand retainer, fifty dollars a day, and expenses?' Bertha asked.

'Right,' Adams said.

Bertha said, 'Retainers are payable in advance before we even start in.'

Adams took out a billfold, smiled and said, 'You mean before I leave the office?'

He gravely counted out ten one-hundred-dollar bills and said to Bertha, 'Make the receipt to the Continental Divide Insurance and Indemnity Company.'

Bertha's diamonds glistened as her greedy fingers hauled in the money, then pulled out a receipt and started scribbling.

I said, 'Expenses will be vouched for, but they're going to be high.'

'How come?'

'If this is crooked – and you have a pretty good idea it is or you wouldn't be spending this much money – these people will be suspicious. They'll check on every answer they get. I'll have to have a complete secondary identity, place of residence, automobile – everything.'

He said, 'Keep the expenses down as much as you can. Get a good secondhand automobile at a bargain price and then you can sell it when you get done with the case, so that we won't be out too much for the car.'

'Does the "we" mean what I think it means?' I asked.

'What's that?'

'That several insurances have got together on this thing and picked your company to make the contact because it was a smaller company and apparently could drive a better bargain?'

He said with dignity, 'You had better take it that the "we" was simply an editorial plural. Your worry will be in doing a good job, not in trying to read my mind.'

Adams took his receipt from Bertha Cool – didn't even bother to glance at it but folded it and pushed it in his pocket.

'I'd like to have prompt action. It's something that has to be handled right now,' he said.

I nodded.

Adams bowed, smiled to Bertha Cool and started for the door.

'Where do I send reports?' I asked.

'You keep in touch with Mrs. Cool, and I'll keep in touch with her,' Adams said, and stalked out.

Bertha held her stubby forefinger to her lips until we heard the outer door close; then the smile broadened all over Bertha's face.

'Now, Donald,' she said, '*this* is the kind of business that gives an agency that aura of respectability which is so hard to come by yet means so much in terms of prestige.'

I didn't say anything.

Bertha went on. 'So many of the cases that *you* take turn out to be assignments where you get mixed up with the lower element – the criminal class. Now here's a case where we're dealing with a man of eminent respectability.'

I feigned surprise. 'You mean you've looked him up already?'

The smile came off Bertha's face. 'He radiates respectability,' she snapped.

'What department is he in?' I asked. 'The claims department, the legal department, or . . . ?'

'He didn't say.'

'What does his card say?'

Bertha opened a drawer and took out a card that was embossed with brilliant blue ink.

'It simply gives the name of the insurance company, and down in the left-hand corner it says "Barney Adams".'

'What's the home address of the insurance company?' I asked.

'Hachita, New Mexico,' Bertha said. 'That's a nice name, isn't it?'

'It's a nice name.'

Bertha said, 'You get the impression of a big company located out there in the open spaces, where there's lots of fresh air, lots of room for parking. I suppose a lot of their business is done by mail.'

'It would have to be,' I said.

'What do you mean?'

'Have you ever been to New Mexico?'

'Yes, lots of times.'

'Ever been to Hachita?'

'No, I don't believe I have. But I know generally where it is.

'Where?'

'Down around Lordsburg somewhere.'

'I've been there,' I told her.

I walked over to the wall, took down the big atlas we had, opened it, looked up Hachita.

I grinned at Bertha Cool. 'Hachita, New Mexico,' I said, 'is given a population of one hundred and forty-two.'

Bertha was bound to have the last word. Her jaw stuck out belligerently. 'That's an old atlas,' she said.

'So it is,' I told her. 'Let's make it a hundred and forty-three.'

Her face darkened.

'Even if it's doubled in population,' I went on, 'it's only two hundred and eighty-four.'

'Well, it's an expensive card!' Bertha snapped.

'Exactly,' I said.

'What do you mean by that crack?' she asked.

'That it couldn't have been printed in Hachita,' I said, and walked out.

CHAPTER TWO

THE apartment I got wasn't exactly what I had had in mind. It was in a third-rate apartment house, but there was a telephone booth at the end of the hall on each of the three floors. The furnishings were old and a little musty, and there was the odor of cooked cabbage clinging to the poorly ventilated hallways.

I had better luck on the car, picking up what looked to be a really good buy at less than Blue Book.

I wrote a letter, giving my new address, to Box 685, drove down to the newspaper and delivered it.

The letter gave the number of the telephone booth on the third floor of the apartment house. My letter had said I would be at that number promptly at ten o'clock that night and at eleven o'clock the next morning.

I signed the letter with my real name, Donald Lam. I had a hunch they'd want to see my driver's license and I didn't have time to get a set of phony credentials.

On the other hand, it's basic policy with a good detective never to let his name and address get listed in a telephone book: so if they tried to look up Donald Lam, they would find nothing.

If they had looked up detective agencies, they would have found a *Cool and Lam*, and that might have been a give-away, but there were a lot of detective agencies in the city – and, anyway, it was a chance I had to take.

I made no attempt to cover the phone at ten o'clock but went home and went to bed. However, the next morning at eleven o'clock I was out in the corridor and when the phone rang I answered it within a matter of seconds.

It was a feminine voice, crisp, businesslike. 'Mr. Lam?'

'Yes.'

'You answered an ad we had in the . . .?'

'That's right – about the accident.'

'You think you could put us in touch with a witness?'

I let my voice show I was playing the cards close to my chest. 'There's a reward in case I do?'

'If you will study the wording of the ad, you will notice that there is a reward if you can produce a witness and if the witness can give the testimony mentioned in the ad.'

'I think you've got a customer,' I told her.

'A customer?'

'Well,' I explained hastily, 'I mean I think I can . . . Yes, I'd better talk with you.'

'Very well, Mr. Lam. Where are you now?'

I gave her the address.

'Promptly at twelve-thirty o'clock this afternoon, you will be at Room Sixteen twenty-four, Monadnock Building. Go right into Sixteen twenty-four and sit down. I will see you just as soon as possible. Be sure you are there promptly at twelve-thirty.'

'I'll be there,' I promised, and hung up.

I drove my car down to a parking lot near the place I was to be at later and looked around a bit.

The Monadnock Building was one of the older office buildings. The elevators rattled a bit. The tile floor in the lobby of the building was a little uneven. The newsstand wasn't very efficiently arranged: cigars, tobaccos, paper-back books were all mixed in a merchandising hash. Maga-zines were in a display rack and also stacked in piles on the floor at the foot of the display rack. The place wasn't too well illuminated.

I decided not to take a chance on going up to look the place over in advance, because the old-fashioned elevators had operators and I didn't want to have anyone remember me as having been in earlier.

I went back out, walked around awhile, came back promptly at twenty-three minutes past twelve, and took the elevator to the sixteenth floor.

Room 1624 was an office with half-a-dozen different names on the door. None of the names meant anything to me.

I went in, and a woman at a desk smiled impersonally and handed me a card. 'Will you please fill out your name and address and the nature of your business?'

I put down my name, the address of the dummy apartment, and wrote 'Answering newspaper ad'.

'Oh, yes,' the woman at the desk said, 'Mr. Lam. I believe you have an appointment for twelve-thirty.'

She consulted her wrist watch, smiled and said, 'I have five minutes to twelve-thirty.'

I nodded.

'Would you mind sitting down and waiting, Mr. Lam?'

'Not at all.'

I had been there about three minutes when the outer office door opened and a woman in her twenties took a couple of steps into the room, then paused and looked to the left and right.

It wasn't exactly the pause one makes in appraising surroundings. It was the pause one makes when trying to decide whether to go ahead with something or to get the hell out of there.

The woman at the desk smiled the same impersonal smile. 'Good afternoon,' she said.

The young woman in the doorway squared her shoulders and marched up to the desk.

The woman handed her one of the cards. 'Will you please write your name, address and the nature of your business?'

I watched the girl filling out the card. Then the woman at the desk said, 'Oh, yes, Miss Creston, you have an appointment for twelve forty-five. You're early . . . quite early.'

The girl laughed nervously. 'Yes, I . . . I'm not fully familiar with the city and I didn't want to be late. I . . .'

'Well, would you mind sitting down and waiting, or would you prefer to come back?'

'Oh, I'll sit and wait.'

The woman started for a chair on my side of the room, then changed her mind and went over and sat across from me.

I had several minutes to look her over. There was nothing else to look at except the desk and a row of chairs on each side of the room. It might have been a waiting room in a doctor's office, only there were no tables with magazines – nothing except the two rows of chairs and the receptionist at her desk.

I looked Miss Creston over.

She had nice legs, wavy chestnut hair, and she was jittery.

A good detective should know something about women's clothes, but that was a branch of my profession on which I needed a lot of coaching.

This girl was wearing clothes that seemed to have been designed for business or travel, and somehow they looked as though they had been traveled in rather extensively. The first spring had gone out of the material, which I gathered had originally been fairly expensive; but the outfit she wore was all well matched – a long topcoat of the same gray material as the two-piece suit beneath – and there was a touch of bright-red scarf at the neck. Her shoes and purse matched in some sort of snakeskin and were the same brownish red as her hat and gloves.

I could see she was interested in me – not, apparently, as another human being, but perhaps as a source of potential trouble.

She looked at me from time to time with quick nervous glances, as though she might be looking over her shoulder apprehensively.

The door from the inner hallway opened and the young woman gave a convulsive start.

A suave-appearing man with a brief case said, 'All done in Twelve A, Miss Smith.'

The woman at the reception desk nodded, smiled, picked up a telephone and said something I couldn't hear.

The man who was all finished in 12A withdrew and the automatic doorstop clicked the door softly shut behind him, and the woman at the reception desk said, 'You may go in for your appointment, Mr. Lam,' and then smiled at the girl and said, 'It will only be a few minutes, Miss Creston.'

'Thank you. I'll wait,' she said.

I walked on past the desk. The receptionist handed me a little slip and said, 'Third room to the right.'

I looked on the slip of paper. It had the number 12A.

I opened the door to the inner offices. There were six of them – three on each side of a little corridor.

I walked down to 12A, the last room on the right, and opened the door.

A dark-complexioned, big-bodied man with oily hair appraised me with eyes that were as cold and hard as those of Bertha Cool.

'Mr. Lam?' he asked.

'Yes.'

'Sit down.'

The office was a little cubicle with an interoffice telephone, a desk, a swivel chair, two straight-backed chairs, some pictures on the wall, and nothing else.

The man behind the desk said, 'My name is Rodney Harper, Mr. Lam. I'm very glad to meet you. You wrote us that you had seen our ad in the paper.'

'That's right.'

'And that you thought you could give us information about a witness?'

'Right.'

'Could you tell us a little more about the witness?'

'He's someone I know.'

Harper smiled. 'Naturally,' he said.

He was a big man, with big hands which rested on the

desk in front of him. There was a desk set with a couple of penholders on the desk, a blotter, an empty pad of paper and the telephone.

I said, 'There's a reward offered?'

'There's a reward offered,' he said. 'Now, I'll have to explain certain things to you at this time so that there will be no possibility of a misunderstanding.'

Harper bent down, opened a brief case, took out a map, spread it on the desk, then took two little plastic automobiles from the brief case and put them on the map.

The map was a large-scale diagram of the intersection of Gilton Street and Crenshaw. They were plainly labeled.

'Now, then,' Harper said, 'this car is a Ford Galaxie that was coming down Gilton Street. You'll remember there's a traffic signal at that street, Mr. Lam.

'At the time of the accident, the Cadillac was coming along Crenshaw Street, and the Galaxie was coming down Gilton Street at high speed. The traffic signal was on amber from the Gilton Street side as the car approached, and the car evidently made a desperate attempt to get across the street before the amber light changed. However, the amber light had very definitely changed to red by the time the Galaxie was at the intersection. It was going too fast to stop.

'It came into the intersection at high speed and hit the Cadillac.'

I said nothing.

Harper moved the car which represented the Cadillac going down Crenshaw. 'Now,' he said, 'this is the Cadillac coming down Gilton. There was a car stopped here in the right-hand lane. The Cadillac was coming in the left-hand lane and was getting ready to stop for the red signal. But, just before the Cadillac got to the intersection, the signal changed to green, so the driver of the Cadillac went on into the intersection.'

'Did he see the Ford?' I asked.

Harper was a little indefinite. 'He was looking at the green light,' he said, 'and he went on into the intersection with the green light. Then this Ford, which was driven heedlessly through the red light into the intersection, came up on his left, traveling at high speed.'

'Where was the Cadillac hit?' I asked.

'Now that, of course, is the embarrassing part,' Harper said. 'The Cadillac was going at a fair speed through the green light at the intersection. And then suddenly the driver saw this Ford and slammed on his brakes. The Ford, however, in place of putting on brakes, speeded up and tried to shoot ahead of the Cadillac and . . . well, it was the Cadillac, actually, that hit the Ford. At the time of the collision, the Cadillac was almost stopped.'

'I see,' I said.

'Now, the fault is plainly with the driver of the Ford automobile.'

'Oh, yes,' I said.

'You have a witness to the accident?' Harper asked.

I said, 'You mentioned a reward.'

'That's right. A reward of three hundred dollars.'

'All I have to do is produce the witness?'

Harper tapped his finger on the map. 'You have to produce a witness,' he said, 'who is prepared to testify that the Ford ran through the red light directly into the intersection and was responsible for the accident.'

'I see,' I said, and was silent.

'You think you know of such a witness?' Harper asked.

'Yes.'

'Well, we'd like very much to talk with him. And, of course,' Harper said with an affable smile, 'it will be to your interest to produce the witness and bring him in here.'

'In that event, when would I get the three hundred dollars?'

Harper was very definite on that point. '*After* you have produced the witness,' he said. '*After* we have talked with him and learned that his testimony is accurate; *after* he has made an affidavit as to what happened.'

'And then I get the three hundred dollars?'

'Then you get the three hundred dollars.'

'Suppose he doesn't testify your way?'

'Tut, tut,' Harper said. 'Not *my* way, young man. I want him to testify to things as they are – to what actually happened. I have told you what happened. We know what happened. We have statements from the driver who is our insured. We naturally wouldn't pay you three hundred dollars for producing a witness whose memory was inaccurate or who was perhaps tied up with the other side of the case.'

'No, I suppose not,' I said. 'But suppose I bring in my witness and something happens and you don't pay off.'

'I am a man of my word, Mr. Lam.'

'It seems I should have something in advance.'

'We can't pay out money for finding a witness before the witness has been found.'

'Suppose *I* am the witness. Would I still get the reward?'

He frowned. 'That's a perplexing question. You gave me no prior intimation that such was the case. In fact, your questions indicated *you* had no first hand knowledge of the accident.'

'I wanted to find out your attitude,' I said.

'Are you a witness?' he asked abruptly.

'Would I get the three hundred dollars if I am?' I countered.

He teetered in his swivel chair for a few moments, then said, 'Well, let me talk with my superiors, Mr. Lam, and then you can be available. Perhaps you'd better call me at three o'clock this afternoon at this number. Now, this number I am giving you isn't the number of the office here, but it's a number where I can be reached.'

He scribbled seven figures on a sheet of paper, tore the sheet of paper from the pad, folded it, got to his feet, shook hands, presented me with the piece of paper and said, 'Until three o'clock then.'

'Three o'clock,' I said, and went out.

I hadn't cleared the door before the receptionist said, 'You may go in, Miss Creston. Room twelve A, the last room on the right.'

I took the elevator down to the lobby, bought a pack of cigarettes at the tobacco counter, walked out to the sidewalk and killed time pretending to be looking at the window display of a sporting-goods stores, mingling with the lunch-hour crowds, trying to be as inconspicuous as possible.

It was about twenty minutes later that she came out.

I followed her for a block and a half.

She turned into the lobby of the Travertine Hotel, walked directly to one of the overstuffed leather chairs which faced the window, and sat down facing the street. She had that air of overpositive assurance adopted by people who aren't at all sure of themselves and expect to be called to task at any time.

I took up a position on the sidewalk where I could see without being seen and waited for the clerk to ask her courteously what her room number was, what she was doing there and so forth, and then let her know in a tactful way that the lobby was reserved for guests of the hotel.

At the end of another fifteen minutes, I was tired of standing on my feet and tired of waiting. I knew that I might be tipping my hand, but I had a feeling this girl was occupied with troubles of her own.

I walked in through the door to the hotel, looked around the lobby, let my eyes fall on her, grow wide in recognition, and said, 'Why, hello!'

She gave me a dubious smile. 'Hello,' she said.

I made quite a point of looking around the lobby, apparently searching for someone who wasn't there, then let my eyes drift back to hers.

She was staring at me with curiosity and a little trepidation.

I moved over toward where she was sitting and said, 'Had a friend supposed to meet me here for lunch. I'm late, and I guess he decided not to wait. I . . . gosh, I know I know you, but I can't remember where we met before.'

She laughed and said, 'We didn't *meet.*'

I registerd indignation. 'Don't tell me that,' I said. 'I know you just as well. I've seen you – not too long ago. We . . . oh,' I said, and my voice trailed off into silence.

Her laughter was musical. 'You've got it now?' she asked.

'I've got it now,' I said. 'You were at that office up in the Monadnock Building. I was sitting looking across at you for several minutes. . . . Say, don't think I'm trying to be fresh. I came in here looking for my friend, and your face was familiar and . . . gosh, I'm sorry.'

'You don't need to be,' she said.

'You're staying here?' I asked.

'I . . . I was waiting for a friend.'

I looked at my watch and said, 'Well, I've missed my appointment all to pieces. I'm twenty minutes late and my friend makes it a point not to wait for anybody . . . Had lunch?'

I made it sound so casual that it would, I hoped, make the question appear sufficiently innocent.

'No,' she said. 'I was going to lunch with my friend but I guess I've missed her.'

'They have a fine merchant's lunch in the dining room here,' I said. 'My friend and I eat here quite frequently and it's really a good place. Since we both lost a luncheon date, let's eat together.'

I kept all anxiety out of my voice, made the invitation sound as casual as though Emily Post had given the procedure the benefit of her blessing.

Her hesitation was just enough to disguise eagerness. 'Well, I . . . I guess perhaps I've missed my appointment . . . I was to be here shortly after twelve-thirty, but I was detained on a business matter . . . you know, up there in the office . . . and I didn't get out until just a few minutes ago.'

'No doubt about it,' I said; 'your friend has thought there was a misunderstanding and gone on. Let's eat.'

I turned casually toward the dining room and she joined me.

'Hungry?' I asked.

'Actually,' she said, 'I'm starved. I had a very light breakfast.'

'Tell you what let's do,' I said. 'If my friend should come here and find me in the dining room with you, he'd claim that I had it all planned that way; and if your friend should come, it might be embarrassing. Let's go down the street about a block to the Steak House.'

'The Steak House?' she asked.

'Most wonderful steaks in the world,' I said, holding up my thumb and finger about an inch and a half apart. 'Extra-thick New York cuts or filet mignons, baked potatoes that are out of this world, onion rings and a nice crisp green salad and ... '

'Don't,' she said. 'My figure!'

'Won't hurt your figure at all,' I said. 'This food is non-caloric.'

'Yes, particularly,' she said, 'the baked potato.'

'With lots of butter melted into it.' I said, 'and paprika on top. And they make some wonderful garlic toast, a concoction of cheese, butter and garlic all melted into ...'

'I have a business appointment this afternoon.'

'If you drink a good wine,' I said, 'it will neutralize the garlic.'

She laughed. 'What a salesman you are. What's your name?'

'Donald,' I said. 'Donald Lam.'

'Mine's Daphne Creston.'

'Miss or Mrs.?'

She said, 'It's going to be Miss from now on. Actually, it's Mrs. My husband walked out on me.' Her voice became filled with bitter sarcasm. 'My dear, darling, devoted husband is all tied up with another woman and left me without a' – she caught herself hastily and finished lamely – 'care in the world.'

Then she went on hurriedly. 'It isn't easy for a person to get by where you have to explain your marital status, so I'm just taking my maiden name back.'

'And shifting for yourself?' I asked.

'That's right.'

At the entrance to the Steak House, she held back a bit. 'Donald,' she said, 'this looks frightfully expensive.'

'Well, it isn't cheap,' I admitted. 'You don't get food like they serve here at bargain-basement prices.'

'But . . . is it all right? I mean, can you afford it? I can't go Dutch in this place.'

I laughed the carefree laughter of reassurance and said, 'Who said anything about Dutch? Just don't look at the right-hand side of the menu. Cover it up; look at the left-hand side; tell the waiter what you want, and it'll be all right.'

'Donald,' she said, 'you certainly are happy and carefree . . . It's going to be midafternoon before we finish. Don't you have a job?'

'My job is working for me,' I said, 'and I'm one of the most indulgent employers you ever encountered. I think nothing of giving a faithful employee like me the afternoon off, particularly when he's having lunch with a beautiful young woman. I find that it improves the morale of the personnel to encourage them in these little dissipations.'

She laughed and said, 'Well, I've got an appointment at four o'clock, but until then I'm free; and the way I feel, I'm just as apt as not to spend the intervening time eating.'

'Wonderful,' I said.

The headwaiter deferentially escorted us to a booth for two. I ordered cocktails and appetizers; soup; a couple of extra-thick filet mignon steaks, medium rare; baked potatoes; green salad; onion rings; garlic bread; a bottle of Guinness stout for myself and some red wine for Daphne.

The cocktails were delicious and were served almost immediately. Daphne ate the appetizers with a relish she didn't try to disguise.

We had vegetable soup, then a small green salad; and then the steaks came on, sizzling hot and cooked to perfection. The steak knives were razor sharp. As they cut into the steaks, the red juices spurted out to form little pools on the plates.

I took a piece of garlic bread and shamelessly sopped the bread in the steak gravy.

Daphne followed suit.

I had my stout; Daphne had the wine I had ordered – wine of a special vintage which I felt certain she would appreciate.

Gradually the color came back into her cheeks.

She tucked away every scrap of food that was on her plate, had two pieces of garlic bread, finished up the small bottle of wine, settled back and smiled.

'My,' she said, '*that* tasted good!'

I said, 'Were you up in that office in the Monadnock Building on the same errand I was?'

'You mean about the accident?'

'Yes.'

She hesitated a moment, then said, 'Yes.'

'That was a peculiar accident,' I said. 'Where were you standing?'

'I was standing on Gilton,' she said.

'You know that the signal changed before the Ford went through?'

'Oh, yes. I was trying to hurry to get across the street, but the signal changed to amber when I was still some distance away and it changed to red before I got to the intersection.

'The Ford *may* have started on the last of the amber, but the signal was red before the Ford ever got across the line into the intersection. He was going fast trying to beat the red light.'

I nodded. 'Got your three hundred bucks?' I asked.

'Not yet. I signed an affidavit. Mr. Harper is going to take it up with his superior. I'm to be back at four o'clock this afternoon. If they use me as a witness, I'm going to get the three hundred dollars.'

'That wasn't the way the ad read,' I said. 'The ad read that they would give three hundred dollars reward for anyone giving information resulting in *locating* a witness.'

'Well, of course,' she said, 'I didn't comply technically. I didn't give them information. I witnessed the accident.'

The waiter hovered inquiringly over the table.

'How about some pineapple sherbet?' I asked Daphne.

She smiled and said, 'I might just as well go all the way.'

I nodded at the waiter. 'Two pineapple sherbets, and then the demitasse.'

We had the sherbet, lingered over the coffee.

'You still have a little time to kill,' I told her. 'Any particular program?'

'No, I'm free until four o'clock.'

I said, 'Where are you staying, Daphne?'

She started to say something, caught herself, looked me in the eye and said, 'I'll be frank with you, Donald. I just came. I parked my bags in a locker at the bus depot. That's only a few blocks, and I'm going back and get them after I have a place to stay.'

'Can I help you? I have a car and . . .'

'Oh, that would be wonderful! And if you could get me a place to stay – I don't want an expensive hotel. I don't know just how long I'll be in town. . . . I'm looking for work, Donald.'

I leaned slightly forward, caught her eyes, and said, 'And you're flat broke.'

Her eyes shifted for a moment of swift panic, and then she turned back and looked straight at me.

'And I'm flat broke,' she admitted.

'And,' I told her, 'you were a good many miles away from here on April fifteenth at the time of that accident. You didn't see it, but you *did* see the ad in the paper.

'You were desperate. You were coming to the city to find work. You looked through the ads to see what you could find.

You saw this ad and thought there was a chance to pick up three hundred dollars by making a bluff and saying that you had seen the accident and . . .'

'Stop it, Donald!' she said. 'Don't read my mind that way. You terrify me!'

'Suppose you tell me a little about yourself.'

'There isn't too much to tell,' she said. 'I am a pretty fair secretary – that is, I used to be. I can do shorthand; I can do dictating-machine work; I am reasonably fast and quite accurate. I had a very fine job, and this Prince Charming came along and – all right, I fell for him. I listened to a wonderful siren song. That man can charm the birds out of the trees. I married him. I gave him what money I had and transferred all my savings into a joint account.

'Then something happened and I became suspicious. I started checking. The man was married, had a wife and a small daughter and had never been divorced. He was keeping them in another home he had here in Los Angeles, and . . . all right, I lost my head. I let him know what I knew. The next morning he was gone. He'd cleaned out the joint bank account.'

'You can get a man like that for bigamy,' I said.

'And what good does that do?' she asked. 'He'll go into court and talk the judge out of doing anything. He'll tell how repentant he is, how he wants only to go back to his legal wife and make a home for his child. The judge will give him probation – and, even if he doesn't, what good is it going to do me to have the guy serving time in a penitentiary?'

'How long did you live with him?'

'About six months. He was, of course, away a lot of that time. He told me he was a manufacturer's representative and had to be on the road a lot of the time.'

'What about getting your old job back?'

She shook her head emphatically. 'It was in a Midwestern city, and the girls in the office all envied me. I tell you this man really had a front. He could impress people. I was so proud of him! I told everyone how I had waited until just the right man came along. No spur-of-the-moment, marry-in-haste-repent-at-leisure stuff for me!'

'Those girls were all so downright envious, I just couldn't bear the thought of letting any of them find out what had actually happened to Daphne Creston's fine marriage.'

'Does the first wife know about you?' I asked.

'I don't think so. I found out about her; there's a seven-year-old daughter.'

'What's his name?' I asked.

She shook her head.

'You might as well tell me. You've told me this much. His name wouldn't mean anything to me.'

'Why do you want to know, Donald?'

'Just in case I should ever meet the guy. I'd know enough to be on my guard.'

She shook her head.

'You still love him,' I charged.

'I hate his guts!'

'Then why did you come to Los Angeles and why are you trying to protect him?'

'I'm not trying to protect him!'

'Have it your own way,' I said, and was silent.

She was uneasy at my silence.

'I took all the money I could scrape up and bought a ticket here and traveled by bus,' she went on after a moment or two. 'I arrived here hungry and dirty. I need a bath. I need to change my clothes and . . .'

'And you came here because you wanted to plead with him to take you back,' I interrupted.

'Plead with him, hell!' she blazed. 'The no-good louse won a hundred and twenty thousand dollars in the Irish Sweepstakes and had his name and picture in all the papers.

'So I *had* to come here so I can send cards to the girls in the office where I worked. Those cards have to have a Los Angeles postmark because the newspapers said he was living here.

'I can't let the girls in the office think I'm high-hatting

them, and I have too much pride to even let them suspect the truth.

'And somewhere, somehow, a purse snatcher got my purse out of my bag, lifted all the money and then returned the purse. I didn't discover what had happened until I got here.

'I'm broke, Donald, flat broke.'

'Go to him, make him give you a stake,' I said.

'I wouldn't ask him for a glass of water if I was dying of thirst in the middle of the Mojave Desert.

'You know what I'm planning to do? If I can't get a job, I'm going to sell myself until I can get one. I'm broke – flat broke!'

I left a bill for the waiter.

'Come on,' I said.

'Where?' she asked.

'I have an apartment,' I told her. 'It's near here. It's not too swanky, but I'll take you there and leave you the key. You can go in and have a steaming-hot tub bath. While you're doing that, I'll get your suitcases out of the locker at the depot. If you hurry, you'll have time to go up and keep your four o'clock appointment. Were you to call personally or to telephone?'

'To call personally.'

'All right,' I said. 'You can . . .'

'No, I can't, Donald,' she said. 'I couldn't do anything like that. After all, you're – well, you're *almost* a stranger.'

'You were talking about selling yourself to strangers,' I said. 'The door of my apartment has a bolt. You can lock it on the inside. I'll give you ten minutes to soak in a good hot tub bath, ten minutes to dress. All I ask in return is that you clean up the bathroom when you leave.'

That did it – that plus the fact that the soak in a hot tub bath appealed to her almost as much as the steak.

She smiled and said, 'It's awfully kind of you, Donald. I'm afraid I'm taking an unfair advantage.'

'No advantage, and nothing unfair about it,' I told her. 'You need a place to bathe and change. Then when you finish up this afternoon you'll have three hundred bucks which you can use as a stake.'

She sighed. 'I certainly *can* use that bath,' she said.

I got my secondhand car out of the parking lot, drove her to my apartment, showed her the towels.

'All right,' I said, 'it's all yours until I get back with the baggage. That bolt on the inside of the door locks the . . .'

'I hate to keep you out of your own apartment, Donald.'

'It's all right,' I told her. 'It's all yours until I get back. Then I'll be up and knock on the door and you can open it for the baggage, and I'll drive you to your four o'clock appointment as soon as you dress.

'And then,' I went on as she hesitated, 'you'll have completed your arrangements, you will have three hundred dollars in cash, and that will serve as a stake until you can get a job. The lawsuit over the collision of the automobiles will be compromised on the strength of your affidavit and you'll never have to get on the witness stand.'

'Oh, I hope so,' she said, 'I . . . I doubt if I could possibly go through with it, but . . . I did this whole thing on impulse after I saw that ad in the paper. I was down to bedrock. It was either that or . . .'

'Sure thing,' I said as she hesitated. 'You had to play it that way. You have no choice. Good heavens girl, suppose you *had* tried to get a night's lodging by dating some man. The city is crawling with fly-cops. Suppose you had been picked up for prostitution. Then what? Wouldn't *that* have been something for the girls in your office to have read about!'

She caught her breath. 'I never thought about that,' she said.

'I'm thinking about it for you,' I said. 'Give me the key to the baggage locker. I've got to hurry.'

She gave me the key.

'How about you, Donald?' she asked. 'Did you see the accident?'

I said, 'I thought I might be able to dig up a witness

who saw it – that was the man I was to have lunch with. But we haven't any time to go into that now if you're going to get all cleaned up. And be sure to get that bathtub clean!'

She laughed and said, 'I'm an excellent housekeeper, Donald.'

'I'm on my way,' I said. 'When I knock, open the door a crack and I'll slide your suitcases inside.'

'Thanks, Donald – for everything!' She had started taking off her clothes even before I had the door closed.

I listened for a moment to see if she turned the bolt on the inside of the door, but I didn't hear it.

The bus depot wasn't far, but I took a cab so I wouldn't have a parking problem. I went to the locker, fitted the key, got out a very good looking suitcase and overnight bag, and had the cab rush me back.

I knocked on the door.

'It's not locked,' Daphne called.

I opened the door.

She was holding a towel around her, looking all fresh and steamy. 'Oh, Donald, you're a dear!'

I smiled, said, 'You'd better hurry,' put the suitcase inside, and backed out of the apartment.

She was smiling as I closed the door.

'You'll be back?' she called to me.

'In ten minutes,' I promised.

I went down to the telephone at the end of the corridor.

I called the number Harper had given me.

He answered the phone right away.

'Mr. Harper,' I said, 'this is Donald Lam. I was to call you at three o'clock. I'm sorry to be a little late. You were going to give me an answer.'

'Yes, Mr. Lam.'

'You have the answer?'

'Yes, Mr. Lam.'

'What is it?'

'I'm sorry,' he said. 'You impress me as being a very estimable young man, but my superiors don't feel the same way.

about you that I do. They feel that you hadn't really witnessed the accident at all but were simply anxious to make three hundred dollars and were willing to testify to the required facts in order to get the money.

'Now, don't blow your stack, Lam! Hear me out. I simply acted as a go-between in the matter. I reported to my superiors. There's a lawyer in this deal who leans over backwards. He insisted that it would be suborning perjury to pay a witness in return for false testimony. I'm terribly sorry it turned out this way, but it's my duty to report facts.'

'How could you give him a statement of our conversation?' I asked. 'I . . .'

'With a tape recorder, of course,' he interrupted. 'I had a concealed tape recorder. Remember the desk set of the two pens? It had a concealed microphone in it, and I let my superiors listen to the tape recording. As I say, this one attorney is a stickler for legal ethics and he felt that you – well, he listened to the tape recording twice and said that you should have told me frankly that you were a witness right at the start if you had actually seen the accident. But your questions, the tone of your voice, and – well, that's the way it is, Mr. Lam. I'm afraid the decision is final. But thank you for calling, and thank you for the interest you took in the matter. Goodbye.'

He didn't wait for me to say anything but hung up the phone at his end.

I went down and sat in my car for ten minutes, then I went back up to the apartment and tapped on the door.

Daphne threw it open. She looked fresh as a daisy and exuded self-confidence.

'Oh, Donald,' she said, 'I feel so much better. This was a wonderful thing – a nice steak, a hot bath, clean clothes. . . . Do we have time to get there at four o'clock? I want to be sure – absolutely sure to be there and . . .'

'Come on,' I told her.

'What about my baggage, Donald?'

'We haven't time to bother with it now. Leave it here. We'll get it when we come back.'

'You have your key?' she asked. 'There's a spring lock on the door.'

'I have it,' I said.

She laughed. 'I never did shoot the bolt you were talking about, Donald. I see it now above the knob on the door. I . . . I guess I just trusted you.'

'That's what you should do, Daphne,' I said.

I took her down to the automobile, drove to the Monadnock Building, then went on past.

'It's very important,' I warned, 'that we shouldn't be seen together. And you must be very careful in talking with Mr. Harper not to let him know that you know me. That might be fatal.

'There's a parking lot half a block down the street here. I'm going down and wait in the parking lot. Walk down there when you finish with your interview and I'll be waiting in the car. Just stand at the check-out station of the parking lot and I'll spot you.'

'Donald, you're wonderful!' she said. She put her hand over mine, gave it a quick squeeze, jumped out of the car and hurried into the Monadnock Building.

I drove around the block, down to the parking place; checked the car in; told the attendant my wife was doing some shopping and I was waiting for her; and sat there with the car pointing toward the street.

It was twenty-three minutes past four when she showed up. I tapped the horn, started the motor, and drove over to pick her up.

'How was it?' I asked.

'O.K.,' she said, 'only . . . only they didn't give me the three hundred dollars.'

'They have your affidavit, don't they?'

'Yes.'

'Well, why didn't they give you the money?'

'I'm to get it tonight at ten o'clock.'

'Where?'

'It's out in Hollywood somewhere. They'll pick me up at the Monadnock Building. It seems there's some attorney connected with the case who wants to study my affidavit carefully and test it against the physical acts in the case. He's a stickler for ethics and he wants to be absolutely certain that he's dealing with a bona fide witness.'

'And if decides he isn't?'

'I don't know,' she said. 'Then perhaps I won't get the money after all.'

'And if you don't?'

She said, 'If I don't . . .' And I could see her collapse like a punctured tire.

She was silent for a moment, then said, 'Donald, why did you say that? Do you think there's any chance they'd have gone this far and had me sign an affidavit and then not give me the money?'

'I don't know,' I told her. 'I was just asking questions.'

'Donald, that three hundred dollars is going to be every red cent I have in the world. I've got less than thirty-five cents in my coin purse, and that's it. And because I've been counting on this three hundred dollars I didn't go to an employment agency and . . . Of course, there *are* ads in the paper; but unless a girl is mighty lucky, she can waste several days going around from place to place, calling on the telephone, making applications. And then you're apt as not to find out the place has been filled.

'And thirty-five cents isn't even enough for bus fare, even if you read the ads in newspapers that have been discarded in the waiting room at the bus depot – which is how I happened to see this ad in the first place.

'I suppose I'm an idiot taking all my money to try to get away from my past – just as if the wheels of a bus could purge my folly . . . and that contemptible purse snatcher!

'When you spoke to me I was on the point of spending the few cents I had for a hamburger sandwich. I was that hungry and that desperate.

'Donald, these people simply *have* to give me that money. If they try to double-cross me, I'll . . .'

'Careful,' I interrupted.

She lapsed into silence.

After a minute she said, 'Donald, a big city is a terrifying place for a young woman who has no money and no connections.'

'What do you mean – no connections?' I asked.

'Just what I said. I don't know a soul . . .'

'Yes, you do,' I interrupted. 'You *have* a connection; you have me.'

She turned to look at me, then said, 'All right, Donald, I have you. And we may as well put the cards on the table. I'm *very* grateful. I'm down and out and . . . well, you're in the driver's seat.

'I can't begin to tell you how much I appreciate what you've done for me. I'm not a piker, and I *am* truly grateful.'

'It wasn't anything,' I told her. 'And after ten o'clock tonight you'll have three hundred dollars.'

'Donald, what do *you* really know about that accident?'

'I thought I could put them in touch with a witness,' I said. 'But this attorney who keeps in the background must be a pretty stuffy individual. He thought perhaps I was more interested in the three hundred dollars than in the ethics of the case, and they turned me down. Don't *ever* let any person with whom you are talking know that you know me or have talked this over with me.'

'I won't,' she promised; then, after a moment, she said, 'Are you going back – to the apartment?'

'Why not?'

'I . . . all right, Donald, I'll go and get my things packed up and – can you take me out for the ten o'clock appointment?'

'Sure thing.'

'And until then?'

'Got any other place to go?' I asked.

'No.'

'Then you may as well stay in the apartment,' I said. 'I've got some business to take care of. You can stretch out and get a little rest.'

'Donald, are you leaving your apartment just because – because I'm there?'

'I've got things to do,' I told her.

'Donald, you're being a gentleman. You're giving me your apartment. You don't need to, Donald.'

'Forget it,' I told her. 'Things will work out all right.'

We drove back to the apartment. I gave her my extra key.

'Just go in and make yourself at home,' I told her. 'And remember there's a bolt on the door. I think you'd better use it.'

'Donald, I don't want to put you out of your own apartment.'

'You're not.'

'I am, too. Couldn't you . . . I mean, if . . . well . . .'

'Nope,' I told her. 'I'll pick you up at nine-thirty. We'll go out to keep this ten o'clock appointment, and then we can have some ham and eggs.'

Her face lit up. 'By that time, *I* can treat *you*,' she said. 'I'll have the three hundred dollars.'

'It's a date,' I told her.

I saw her as far as the door of the apartment house, then patted her shoulder and drove to the office.

The receptionist was just leaving as I entered. Elsie Brand was at her desk. Bertha Cool was still in the office.

Elsie Brand said, 'Bertha is *very* anxious to see you, Donald. She's been asking every few minutes.'

'O.K.,' I said, 'we'll see what Bertha has on her mind.'

I walked over to Bertha's private office. As soon as I opened the door she said, 'Donald, where the hell have you been?'

'Working on this insurance case.'

'Well, this fellow Adams has been calling up half-a-dozen times this afternoon. He wanted to know if you had established contact. He said to be very, very, very careful – that he had a feeling they were suspicious of you and thought you might be a detective.'

'Who was the "they" he was referring to?'

'The people who put that ad in the paper.'

'All right,' I said. 'Anything else?'

'What do you mean "anything else"? You've seen them, haven't you?'

'Yes.'

'Were they suspicious?'

'I don't know. I had an interview and let them know I'd be receptive, but they turned me down.'

'That's what Adams was afraid of, Donald. They've got you spotted. He was afraid you'd be too direct. He wants a report.'

'I'll contact him after a while,' I said.

'Adams was all worked up,' Bertha went on. 'He felt that we had loused the job up. He left a number for you to call just as soon as I could get in touch with you.'

'O.K., call him now,' I said.

Bertha said, 'He may be rather rough. He said he was very much disappointed and – well, the son of a bitch seemed angry.'

'Let's get him on the phone,' I said. 'You have his number?'

'I have his number.'

Bertha got an outside line, dialed the number, said, 'Mr. Adams?'

Butter wouldn't have melted in her mouth. 'This is Bertha Cool, Mr. Adams. Donald just came in and I told him you wanted to talk with him. Here he is; hold the phone, please.'

I took over the phone, said, 'Hello. This is Donald Lam.'

'What the devil has happened?' Adams said. 'You've loused the job all to pieces!'

'What do you mean I've loused the job?' I asked.

'They've got wise to you in some way.'

'What do you mean they're wise to me?'

'That you're a phony; that you're a private detective.'

'I don't think they have,' I said.

'Well, *I* think they have,' he told me.

'On what do you base your information?' I asked.

He said, 'I base my information on the fact that they have very definitely closed with someone else.'

'What do you mean closed?'

'They have another witness.'

'They didn't say anything in the ad about only one witness.'

'Well, you try and collect for two and see what happens,' Adams said.

'Of course, I can't help it if there were other witnesses,' I told him. 'Thousands of people read those want ads, and someone who saw the accident could very well have . . .'

'Saw the accident, my eye!' Adams stormed. 'That was why I was so anxious to get action. I was afraid they might close the deal with someone else.'

'I had a very nice interview with them,' I said.

'Did you get the three hundred dollars?'

'No.'

'When was the last contact you had with them?'

'About three o'clock. It seems there's some lawyer connected with the case that is so ethical he leans over backwards and . . .'

'Phooey!' Adams interrupted. 'I tell you they brushed you off. You didn't put on the right kind of an act.'

'All right,' I told him. 'Have it your own way. I'm not going to argue with you. Now what do you want me to do?'

'I want my money back.'

'All of it?'

'All of it.'

'There have been quite a few expenses,' I said. 'We don't guarantee results. We guarantee effort and that's all.'

'Look here,' Adams said, 'you try that approach with me and you'll regret it. I represent big business. I gave you a job and you loused it up.'

'I haven't loused it up yet,' I told him.

'Yes, you have. You'll never have any more contact with that outfit. And if you try it, they'll be so suspicious they won't let you get within a mile of them.'

'You know that for a fact?'

'I know it for a fact.'

'All right,' I said. 'Now, I'll ask you a question: *How* do you know it?'

'Don't think I was foolish enough to trust everything entirely to you. I had other contacts.'

'Exactly,' I said, 'and those other contacts are what loused up the job. That's the worst of you amateurs – you want to act like professionals. Just because you're dabbling around with investigations in an insurance company, you think you know all about detective work.

'I wondered who else was butting into the picture. Now I know: it's you. All right, you created a lot of obstacles and made things more difficult for me, but I'll take it in my stride and come out all right. But, from now on, I'm warning you: keep out of the case!'

'You think you still have a chance?'

'There's more than one way to skin a cat,' I told him. 'Of course I have a chance. If I can't get what I want one way, I'll get it another. But you keep out of this, you understand?'

'You can't give me orders!'

'The hell I can't,' I said. 'I'm giving you orders right now! If you don't stay out of it beginning as of now, you're going to be out of luck!

'As it is, you've loused things up, but I think perhaps I can recoup our losses.'

There was a silence for several seconds; then he said, 'I see no reason for your confidence.'

I asked, 'Where can I reach you?'

'Right here at this number.'

'It may be late tonight.'

'You can always reach me through this number.'

'O.K.,' I said. 'Can you give me an address?'

'No, this is an unlisted telephone number. Call me here and I'll answer. But I want you to understand . . .'

'I understand everything,' I told him. 'I took a contract to do a job, and I'm going to do it. But I want you to keep the hell out of it. Now, do you get that?'

He hesitated for two or three seconds, then he said, 'Very well, but don't talk to me like that.'

'Keep out of my way, then,' I told him. 'Just so that's understood, we'll get along.'

I hung up the telephone.

Bertha was watching me with apprehensive eyes. 'You can't talk to a client like that, Donald,' she said.

'The hell I can't!' I said. 'I can and I did. He's one of those guys who won't trust anyone. He hired us to do a job and then he either hired some other agency to check on us or he tried to do it through his own operative. The result of it is that the fat is in the fire and I'm going to have a hard job getting things straightened out.'

'He's an influential businessman,' Bertha said. 'You mustn't antagonize clients that way. You . . .'

'Phooey!' I interrupted. 'I know the type. He's the arrogant, browbeating businessman – the sort of individual who gets you on the defensive and then rides you to death. I don't intend to have him riding me to death.'

'What are you going to do?' Bertha asked.

'Go out on the job and get results,' I told her.

'Do you think you can?'

'I always have, haven't I?'

'You're a smart little bastard,' Bertha admitted grudgingly, 'but I wish you hadn't talked to him that way.'

I leaned over Bertha's desk, copied the telephone number Adams had given her into my notebook, and said, 'It's the only way to talk to him. I think I know how he loused the job up. If he calls you, don't knuckle under to him.'

'Did he want his money back?' Bertha asked.

'He started talking that way.'

Bertha's expression changed. 'Under those circumstances,'

she said, 'we can't afford even to be halfway pleasant to the son of a bitch!'

'Keep that in mind,' I told her, and walked out.

I said good night to Elsie, told her not to worry if she didn't see me for a few days, to keep her mouth shut and be enigmatic to callers. Then I drove to police headquarters, got into the traffic division and started pawing through records. It took a while to find what I wanted but, finally, I found it. On 15th April a Cadillac driven by Samuel Afton had collided with a Ford Galaxie driven by George Bains at Gilton and Crenshaw. Police had made an investigation and had issued a citation to Samuel Afton, driver of the Cadillac, for running a red signal without making a stop and for failing to yield the right of way.

After that I dropped by a friendly newspaper office and looked in the files – the so-called morgue – for the names of the last winners of the Irish Sweepstakes.

The big winner was Dennison Farley. His picture showed him to be a good-looking guy with a big mouth.

I copied his address.

CHAPTER THREE

George Bains was listed in the telephone book. I got him on the phone.

'I know it's an imposition,' I said, 'but I'd like to talk with you for a few minutes about a personal matter. Will you see me if I drive out?'

'What's the name?' he asked.

'Donald Lam,' I told him.

'Oh, all right,' he said. 'Come on out. If you want to make the trip, I'll take a look at you and see how you impress me.'

'Fair enough,' I told him, and hung up.

He lived down at the beach. It took me a while to get out there. The place turned out to be a small apartment. Bains and his wife were in their thirties and apparently had no children.

'All right,' he said; 'what's it all about?'

'April fifteenth means anything to you?' I asked.

He grinned and said, 'What does it mean to *you*?'

'It means something I'm investigating.'

'All right,' he said; 'I was in an automobile accident.'

'What happened?'

'I was driving my automobile along Gilton Avenue, and when I came to the intersection at Crenshaw I slowed for a stop light, but the light changed just as I got there so I moved on through.

'A Cadillac driven by a man named Samuel Afton was coming fast down Crenshaw. I think he tried to beat the red light, saw he couldn't make it, slammed on the brakes, couldn't stop fast enough, and ran into me.'

'What's the status of the litigation?' I asked.

'There isn't any litigation.'

'What's the status of the claim you've made?'

'Paid.'

'You mean Afton has paid off?'

'It was the insurance company that did the paying,' Bains said. 'And I'll say this: their investigator was a nice guy. He came out and got my statement, looked at the damage, asked me if I was hurt, took me to a doctor for a checkup, took my car to the garage, ordered repairs on it, fixed up everything in first-class shape, and came out to see if I was completely satisfied with the car.'

'You were?'

'Yes. It ran like new.'

'How much was the damage?'

'I don't know. The car was damaged pretty much, but the insurance company took care of the whole thing.'

'Know what insurance company it was?'

'Sure,' he said, 'It was the Metropolitan Auto Indemnity Company.'

'Fine,' I told him. 'I was just checking up on some of the insurance companies. I wanted to see how they handled their claims. You're certain this was handled in a manner satisfactory to you?'

'It sure was.'

I thanked Bains and drove back to the apartment.

Daphne Creston was fresh and radiant.

'Donald,' she said, 'I'll be moving out tonight as soon as I get the money, and I do want you to know how much I appreciate all that you've done for me. I've cleaned things up a little bit. Well, I've straightened up the kitchen and on the shelves. It doesn't look as though you've been here very long, Donald.'

'No,' I told her, 'not very long.'

'You have a lot of new provisions that haven't even been opened.'

'I keep them so I can eat here when I need to, but I eat out a lot of the time.'

She regarded me thoughtfully for a moment, then said, 'Well, Donald, it's been fun knowing you, and I want to tell you you're one of the nicest men I've ever known.'

'You've never given anybody the address of this apartment?' I asked.

'Heavens, no. I gave them the address of the hotel where you met me. I intend to get a room there just as soon as I get some money and . . .'

'And no one knows how to get in touch with you?'

'No. I get in touch with them.'

'Now, your instructions tonight are what?'

'I'm to be in front of the Monadock Building at ten minutes to ten on the dot. I'm going to be picked up there and taken to the residence of the attorney, who is going to give me the three hundred dollars. It's out in Hollywood somewhere.'

'Daphne,' I said, 'do something for me.'

'What?'

'Don't go.'

'Don't go, Donald?'

'That's right. Don't go.'

'But, Donald, I'm absolutely flat broke. You know that. I've done the job; I've given them the affidavit. And, as you pointed out, they'll probably use that affidavit to make a settlement and – why, Donald. I'm *entitled* to the money.'

'It's a poor way to make money,' I told her.

'Beggars can't be choosers.'

'To some extent they can. And you're not a beggar.'

'What do you mean by that?'

'You've got a home,' I said.

'Where?'

'Here.'

'Oh, Donald, I couldn't. I ... Why, Donald, you don't *really* mean – or do you mean ...?'

'What?'

'Move in with you.'

'That wasn't what I said. I said you had a home here. I've got a place I can stay.'

'Another place?' she asked.

'It's a place I can stay.'

She came to me and looked searchingly into my eyes. She was angry. 'Donald,' she said, 'are you spending the time with some other girl in her apartment while I'm here?'

'I didn't say that,' I said. 'I said I had another place I could stay. I live in this town, you know. I have friends. You can stay right here until you connect with something; I can give you get-by money, and there's enough groceries in the kitchen to keep you going for a while.'

'I noticed,' she said thoughtfully, and then added, '*New* groceries. The packages haven't been opened – canned goods, frozen foods in the freezing compartment of the refrigerator ... Tell me, Donald, do you really love her?'

I laughed and said, 'That's the way with a woman. She jumps to conclusions. Now, forget this appointment tonight and don't ever go back to those people. Just stay away from them. Then let's keep an eye on them and see what they do next.'

'But, Donald, it's all very obvious. They already have my affidavit. They'll use that to make a settlement with the insurance company, just like you said.'

I said, 'That office up in the Monadnock Building is just a hole in the wall. You can go in there and rent one of the offices by the day, by the week, by the month, or probably by the hour. You can have the office from twelve noon until one o'clock; you can pretend it's your office; all you pay is an hour's rental.

'When you're finished, someone else moves in and pays an hour's rental. Some of them probably rent by the day. Perhaps they have a few customers who rent by the week; but it's a fly-by-night business with the woman out in front running things, collecting rentals; and probably she's a stenographer who furnishes stenographic service when necessary.'

Daphne thought it over, then said, 'Well, if they're just doing temporary investigative work on account of *one* accident, you wouldn't expect them to have a permanent office.'

'Why not? If you're dealing with a reputable insurance company and an attorney at law who is so darned ethical, you'd expect . . .'

'No, Donald,' she interrupted; 'I've gone this far. I'm going to see it through. I'm a young woman who likes to stand on her own two feet. I've appreciated what you've done for me; but I'm not going to sponge on you, and I'm not going to put you out of your own apartment.

'And,' she added after a moment, 'so far, those are the only alternatives you've indicated as possibilities, Sir Galahad!'

She was looking at me with laughing eyes.

'All right,' I told her, 'you're living your own life, but I just have a hunch on this thing. I'm smelling something very, very fishy.'

'Donald,' she said, 'you never have told me about your connection with this.'

'What do you mean "my connection"?'

'You went there to try and collect three hundred dollars. They didn't play ball with you. Do you know why not?'

'No.'

'Donald, tell me – did you see the accident?'

I grinned at her and said, 'I saw the ad in the paper.'

'Do you need money that badly, Donald?'

'I'm a sharpshooter,' I told her. 'I can always pick up a few bucks here and there; and when I see an ad like that, it's a challenge.'

'Donald, I have a peculiar feeling that there's more to this than you're telling me.'

'But you're not going to listen to me?'

'No. And I've got to go.'

'All right,' I told her, 'I'll drive you to within a couple of blocks of the Monadnock and you can walk from there. Now, you stay here tonight. When you come back, you let yourself in; you have a key.'

'And where will you be, Donald?'

'I have another place to stay. I told you.'

'Donald, you could . . . well, what I mean . . . Donald, I simply can't keep putting you out of your place this way and I'm not going to stay here. I've got everything all ready for you to move back in. I'll have three hundred dollars, and I'm going to that little hotel down the street a block and a half from the Monadnock. It's reasonably priced and respectable.'

'Have it your own way,' I told her.

She said somewhat wistfully, 'After tonight, I won't be seeing you again. I'll go my way and you'll go yours. The city will swallow us up. It's unlikely our paths will ever cross again.'

'Well, it's been nice knowing you,' I told her.

She said, 'I don't want to say goodbye to you in an automobile parked on a crowded street a couple of blocks from the Monadnock Building.'

'When do you want to say goodbye to me?'

'Now.'

'Don't you want me to drive you to . . .'

'Of course I do. I'm not talking about that; I'm talking about saying goodbye.'

And with that she put her arms around my neck, held her face close to mine for a moment, said, 'Donald, you're marvelous! You're . . . you're . . . you're just too darned good to be true!

'Here's my thank-you!'

She pressed her lips against mine and gave me a long kiss that started out as a chaste thank-you but speedily went into high gear and stayed there.

When she broke away, she looked at me with starry eyes. 'Donald, I wasn't sure about you, but . . .'

'What do you mean you weren't sure?' I asked.

'I didn't know. You never tried to push things, never tried to take advantage, never made any – well, dammit, you didn't make any passes!'

'Was I supposed to?'

'Of course you were supposed to! Men are supposed to make passes; women are supposed to have the right of selection. They accept the ones they want and dodge the ones they don't want.'

'So you weren't sure of me?'

She laughed and said, 'I was afraid perhaps you were one of those men who . . . who didn't like women.'

'And what do you think now?'

'Good Lord, Donald, you wound me up and started me running! Come on; we've got to go, we've things to do. I was just saying goodbye and thanking you while I had the chance. . . . Now I'm all packed up. If you want me to . . . All right, Donald, you carry the suitcase, I'll carry the overnight bag and coat, and we can leave them at the hotel.'

'And you won't call it off?' I asked.

'No. I've gone this far and I'm going to see it through.'

'All right, let's go,' I told her.

I carried the suitcase and she carried the other stuff down to the car. I put it in the back, drove to the hotel, gave a bellboy a tip and told him to hold the baggage for a couple of hours; then I drove around the block and let Daphne out.

She said goodbye once more, regardless of the people streaming by on the sidewalk, regardless of the fact that we were parked in front of a fireplug with the motor running. It was some goodbye. She came up for air, looked at me speculatively.

'Donald, I get the darnedest feeling about you,' she said in a taut voice.

'What sort of a feeling?' I asked.

'You're holding yourself back. You're holding yourself under wraps. Why? You're a man. Let me make the decisions.'

'What makes you think I'm holding back?'

'You act as though this was some sort of a . . . I don't know – some sort of a business assignment. I thought for a while you were working with the insurance company – a part of the whole setup. But – I just don't know. All I know is that, for some reason, you're holding back.'

'And it bothers you?'

'Of course it bothers me. A girl doesn't like to have the boys hold back. She wants to do the holding. But you've got something way down deep in the bottom part of your mind, something you're working on. I was afraid for a while you weren't human; that you weren't – well, I didn't mean that you weren't human; I meant that you weren't one of the men who appreciated the opposite sex.'

'You've got that out of your mind now?'

She laughed and said, 'I haven't had such a kick saying goodbye for a long, long . . . Heavens, I've got to be there at ten minutes to ten on the dot, and I've got a block and a half to walk! Goodbye, Donald.'

She gave me another hurried kiss, jerked the door open, jumped out to the sidewalk, and quickly walked away.

I let her get well down the street; then I moved the car down to a point where I could see the entrance of the Monadnock Building.

Rodney Harper was there waiting for her. He looked accusingly at his wrist watch when she came up, and I saw her stand close to him and start talking rapidly.

Harper took her elbow, piloted her down the street to the parking lot.

I slid in front of a fireplug and waited for them to come out.

I didn't have long to wait. Harper was doing the driving; she was sitting beside him in a Lincoln Continental.

I swung in behind, got close enough to see that the license place of the Lincoln had been removed. After that I eased back so Harper wouldn't know he was being followed.

I knew that I stood a risk of ranking the whole job; but that was a chance I had to take.

I did a pretty fancy job of tailing. At times I turned my lights down and slid in close to the curb when I was sure of myself and of him. At times I stayed far behind; at times I moved up close.

It was one of the times when I was far behind that I lost them. When I moved up, they were gone.

I circled the block; I cut down side streets; I used every trick I knew, but the big Lincoln was gone. I revised my opinion of Harper. He hadn't been a simpleton; he'd known he was wearing a tail, and he'd waited until his own time to ditch it in the way he wanted it ditched.

I tried methodical thinking, but I was having a little difficulty.

The car couldn't have gone on down the main boulevard. He must have turned either right or left – probably right. He could, of course, have doubled back; but he had probably gone down a side street. If Harper knew he was being followed, he'd have cut corners and done some fancy driving and I was out of luck. If he didn't know he was being followed, it was possible he was parked somewhere nearby.

I had lost him if he was on the move. The only chance I had left was that he was parked. So I drove down the side streets looking in the driveways. Twenty minutes passed. Then, suddenly, I heard a siren. I pulled over to the curb, shut off my headlights.

A police car rocketed past me, going fast, siren screaming.

I cursed myself for letting her go with these chiselers, cursed myself for being so conservative on a tailing job that I lost the car I was tailing, and cursed myself for letting the agency get hooked into this sort of a deal.

I took out after the police, going fast.

It went on down the street for about three blocks, then suddenly splashed into crimson all over the rear end as the driver slammed on the brakes hard and made a turn into a driveway.

I was trapped. There was only one thing for me to do and that was to keep moving.

As I went past the place where the police car had turned in, I tried to catch the house number. As nearly as I could tell, it was 1771; but I had only a brief glimpse. Then I saw officers coming out of the car – one of them running around to the rear door of the house and the other one starting for the front door.

Then I had passed by.

The officers had been intent on what they were doing. They weren't paying attention to my car. I heaved a sigh of relief and gradually started building speed.

Then, suddenly, a siren sounded and a police car swung around the corner two blocks ahead of me, turned in my direction, and started coming fast – red light blinking, siren screaming.

I pulled over to the curb.

I was in a residential district. It was a well-used street. The police car was screaming for the right of way. I had the right to pull over to the curb and stop. In fact, it was my duty to do so under the law; but, under the circumstances, it made me a target.

I saw an officer in the rear seat of the car peering out through the window. Then, suddenly, the brakes went on on the police car.

I pretended I hadn't noticed anything, waited until the car went past, pulled away from the curb and started moving. But it was no use. The police whipped into a U-turn. The siren sounded again, and the red spotlight bathed my car in ruddy brilliance.

Once more I pulled into the curb.

The police car came alongside.

'Just a check,' one of the officers said. 'You have your driver's license and registration slip?'

'What's the big idea?' I asked.

'Just a check,' the officer repeated.

Then the rear door opened. Sergeant Frank Sellers got out, took one look at me and said, 'Well, I'll be a son of a sea cook!'

'Hello, Sergeant,' I said.

'Well, if it isn't Pint Size himself!' Sellers said.

The officer who had asked for my driver's license said to Sergeant Sellers, 'You know this guy?'

'Hell, yes!' Sellers said. 'He's a private eye. He's mixed in more wild-eyed cases than you can shake a stick at. What are you doing down here, Pint Size?'

'I'm working,' I told him.

'Isn't that nice! *What* are you working on down here?'

'I came down here to meet a man.'

'What's his name? Where does he live?'

'I don't know. He told me to cruise along Hemmet Avenue between the seventeen-hundred and one thousand blocks and he'd pick me up.'

'What's his name?'

'I don't know. It was a telephone call.'

'Somebody just told you to come down to Hemmet Avenue at this time of night and cruise around and he'd pick you up. He didn't give you a name, and you jumped in your car and came scooting down here.'

'That's not right, but we'll let it ride at that.'

'I don't believe you.'

'Nobody asked you to.'

'Well, for your information,' Sergeant Sellers said, 'there's been a murder committed at 1771 Hemmet Avenue – that's back here a couple of blocks. Somebody shot a very prominent lawyer. And we come boiling out here in response to a radio call and find you cruising in the neighborhood. Now, *isn't* that a coincidence?'

'Meaning you think I committed the murder?'

'No,' Sergeant Sellers said, 'You're not that dumb. But I wouldn't be at all surprised if the person who did commit it is a client of yours or if you aren't mixed up in the case in some way.'

'Well, I'm not mixed up in it in any way,' I told him.

'You are now,' he told me. 'Get in your car and follow us back to 1771; that's where we're stopping. I'll look the place over and then I'll do some more questioning. Maybe by that time you'll have thought up a more convincing story.'

Sellers climbed back in the police car; I put my car in a U-turn and followed them back to the big house where the first police car had turned in.

I saw then there was another police car back in the driveway and that the car Sergeant Sellers was in made three police cars parked at the place.

Lights were on in adjoining houses, and people began to gather – timid, diffident people, poking their heads out of doors, then coming out to front porches, then walking over the property lines.

Sellers said, 'You wait here, Lam, and don't make any move to get away. Don't try to communicate with anybody. Just stay right there.'

'Am I under arrest or something?'

'We'll put it this way,' Sellers said: 'one false move out of you and you *will* be under arrest.'

'Just because I was driving a car in the neighborhood,' I said bitterly.

'Just because you were driving a car in the neighborhood,' Sellers said, 'and because you're mixed up in more unconventional stuff than any other private detective I've ever met. You're daring; you're ingenious; you're unconventional; and the hell of it is you've got a reputation all over town for being daring, ingenious and unconventional. The result of all that is that people come to you with assignments they wouldn't give to anybody else; and you take them.

'Eventually, that's going to lead to losing your license. One of these days you won't be lucky.'

'You say there's a murder in there?' I asked.

'That's the story. Dale Dirking Finchley – ever heard of him?'

I shook my head.

'He's quite a lawyer, although he doesn't get around court much. He's one of these fellows who plays it behind the scenes. I guess you'd call him a political attorney. Now then, having refreshed your recollection, so to speak, does the name mean anything to you?'

'Not a thing.'

Sellers said, 'And, of course, you'd tell me if it did!'

'Of course,' I echoed.

Sellers grunted, turned away from me and went on into the house.

I sat there and waited.

Officers came and went. I could hear the police radios on the parked cars conveying messages back and forth. After a while, Sellers came out. He walked over to my car. 'Thought up any better story by this time?' he asked.

I said nothing.

'All right, Lam. I'm going to ask you some questions. Now, this is going to be official. I'm investigating a murder case. If you lie to an officer who is investigating a murder case, it consists of giving false evidence. You know what that means.'

'Listen,' I told him, 'just because you're investigating a murder case doesn't mean you have the right to ask a lot of extraneous questions and come prying into the private business of a detective agency, trying to get me to betray the confidences of clients. Now, you ask me any question that is connected in any way with this murder investigation, and if I have any pertinent information I'll give it to you and I'll try not to lie.

'On the other hand, if you ask me questions which would cause me to betray a confidence in regard to my business, and questions which have no bearing on the murder, I'm going to give you some purely synthetic answers.'

'You aren't going to give me any synthetic answers on the questions I ask,' Sellers said. 'Now, I'll ask you first – how long have you been in the neighborhood?'

'I was just cruising. I came down the street directly behind the police car that turned in the driveway. I thought at the time it was the first car, but I see now there was a car ahead of it.'

'That checks,' Sellers said. 'The driver remembered you were coming behind him. Now then, were you alone in the car?'

'I was alone in the car.'

'What were you doing down here?'

'I was looking for a party.'

'Someone who had telephoned you and told you to meet him here?'

I said, 'That story I told you was condensed and slightly edited. The true facts are I'm doing a confidential job for a man who gave me an unlisted telephone number and a retainer.'

'What sort of a job?'

'It has to do with an automobile accident. At least, as far as I know.'

'Do you know if Dale Finchley was working on that case?'

I shook my head. 'I don't know that he was, but I have every reason to assume that he wasn't.'

'Why?'

'Because the case, as such, had been settled and . . .'

'Settled?'

'That's right. Settled out of court.'

'Then why were you investigating it?'

'Because my client wanted me to.'

'And why should he want to investigate a case that had already been settled?'

'That,' I said, 'is one of the things that's bothering me about the case. But I think my client is interested in a whole series of cases, of which this just happens to be one. There's supposed to be an insurance angle, and it just may be that someone has worked out a system of sticking insurance companies.'

'I'd like to have the name of your client,' Sellers said.

'I'm not at liberty to give it to you because, as you can see, it has absolutely nothing to do with this case.'

'But it had something to do with this territory – this neighborhood.'

I said, 'I don't think it did.'

'Then what were you doing here?'

'I'll put it right on the line, Sergeant. I was trying to tail a car. I was afraid the driver was suspicious. I was coming down the boulevard and had every reason to believe we were going on for quite a ways. I dropped far behind so he wouldn't notice my headlights, because it was a one-man trailing job. And I lost him.'

'Where did you lose him?'

'About five blocks back on the boulevard.'

'How did you lose him?'

'I was so far behind, I don't know. A couple of cars were coming toward me, their headlights dazzled me, and when they got past, I couldn't find my man anywhere, I assumed he must have turned off. If he'd speeded up and gone on ahead, I was licked. So I was starting a swing around the residential district here to see if I could pick up the car.'

'What kind of a car?'

I looked him straight in the eye. 'A four-door sedan.'

'Dammit,' Sellers said, 'that isn't what I meant and you know it. What make? If you were tailing the car, you picked up the license number.'

I said, 'If it's connected in any way with the murder case, you may have it. But the car wasn't parked on Hemmet Avenue; it wasn't parked on any of the side streets around here. I've come to the conclusion it went on through. I think the driver knew I was tailing him and speeded up when I dropped so far behind.'

Sergeant Sellers said, 'I'm going to let you get by with it this time, Lam, largely because I can't put my finger on anything specific. But I'll put it right on the line with you: every time you're mixed into a case, you try to protect the interests of your clients without regard for how the police may feel.

'You have the right to represent a client, but the police are in charge of every phase of a criminal investigation, and don't ever forget it.

'Now, get the hell out of here!'

I got out of there.

I couldn't be certain whether I was being followed or not, so I decided to play it safe and drove directly to my regular apartment, without going near the new one I had rented. If Sergeant Sellers was having me tailed, I didn't want to tip him off to that new apartment – not just yet.

CHAPTER FOUR

I RANG the Travertine Hotel at eight o'clock the next morning.

'May I speak to Daphne Creston?' I asked.

'Just a moment, please,' the operator said; then, after a moment, said, 'We don't have a Daphne Creston registered here.'

'Does she have a reservation?' I asked.

'Apparently not.'

'Can you give me the bell captain or whoever is in charge of the baggage room? I want to see if she's left baggage and intends to check in later.'

'Just a moment.'

The operator plugged me in on a new connection; a masculine voice said, 'Hello'; and I said, 'Are you in charge of the baggage room?'

'That's right.'

'Has Daphne Creston called and picked up her things? She left some baggage and . . .'

'No, sir, the baggage is still here.'

'All right,' I told him; 'I guess she'll be in later then. Thank you. Goodbye.'

The Finchley murder had taken place too late for the early editions, but the radio broadcasts had some details.

Finchley, a very prosperous attorney living in a swanky house in the Hollywood-Beverley Hills district, had been engaged in an argument with someone who had shot him through the heart with a .38 caliber revolver and escaped.

A neighbor had heard voices raised in argument, had heard the sound of the shot, and had notified police. Police, in turn, had notified patrol cars by radio, and police were in the house within a matter of minutes. They had found Finchley lying dead on the floor of his second-floor study. There was no sign of his assailant.

Finchley was described as being a wealthy widower, somewhat retiring although his company was much sought by hostesses.

There were no servants in the house at the time of the shooting.

Police found the back door unlocked and standing partially open. The door was equipped with a spring lock, so that it would only have been necessary for anyone leaving the house to have pulled the door shut and the spring lock would have snapped into place.

Since the house was in a quiet residential neighborhood, with houses separated from the street by well-kept lawns, neighbors were not inclined to snoop. The sound of the argument and the pistol shot had been about the only clues unearthed by the police.

One of the neighbors, however, had thought that a car containing one man had been parked for about two minutes in front of the Finchley house with the motor running. This neighbor was walking his dog and wouldn't have paid any attention to the car if it hadn't been for the fact that the motor was running. As it was, he glanced at it casually. He couldn't be certain of the make or model of the car but had gathered a general impression of a youngish-to-middle-aged, well-dressed man sitting in the front seat.

Police felt that Finchley, at the time of his death, had been talking over business matters while seated at his desk in the second-floor study.

The lawyer had been shot at close range, and the absence of any struggle indicated that it was someone the attorney knew, who had been admitted to the house probably in accordance with a prior appointment.

The neighbor who had heard the altercation told police he thought Finchley had said, 'I'm calling your bluff and the pol . . .'

And then came the shot.

The neighbor thought Finchley was going to say he was calling a politician, but it could have been he was about to say he was calling the police.

After the sound of the shot, there had been the sound of a woman's single short scream.

The neighbor hadn't been certain the noise he heard was a door slamming, but the sound, coupled with the woman's scream, had made him decide to call the police.

I went to the office, casually dropped in on Bertha Cool.

'What's new?' I asked.

'Nothing. Did you get in touch with Barney Adams?' I shook my head.

Bertha's face showed irritation. 'He wanted you to call him just as soon as you came in.'

Bertha opened her desk, took out the card with the telephone number Adams had given her, and gave the number to our switchboard operator. 'Get Mr. Adams at that number,' she said.

After a while, Bertha's phone rang.

Bertha gave her hair a quick pat, put a conciliatory smile on her face, picked up the telephone and said, 'Yes, hello,' in her most dulcet voice.

Her expression underwent a swift change. 'The hell he doesn't,' she said. 'You sure you dialed the right number? Yes, that's right.

'Well, he may be out to breakfast. Try him again in about half an hour.'

I said, 'Well, we called. He can't ask for anything more than that.'

'Of course,' Bertha pointed out, 'we don't know what this number is. It's his private apartment, for all we know. We'll try it again in half an hour. You going to be in?'

'I'll be in and out,' I told her.

'How're you coming on the investigation?'

'So-so.'

'What have you uncovered?'

I said, 'I'm not prepared to make a report right now, but I *think* they aren't interested in getting a witness to the accident mentioned in the ad.'

'What!' Bertha exclaimed.

I nodded.

'Don't be silly, Donald! They have to be interested; they're paying three hundred dollars for information leading to the location of a witness.'

'A witness,' I said, 'who will testify that the Ford went through a stop signal and hit the Cadillac.'

'Well, naturally, they aren't going to spend money for an unfriendly witness.'

'Actually,' I said, 'the case is the opposite. The Cadillac went through the signal and hit the Ford.'

Bertha's eyes blinked rapidly while she digested that bit of information. 'No wonder they're willing to pay three hundred bucks,' she said at length.

'And,' I said, 'the case was all settled before the ad was put in the paper.'

Bertha's chair squeaked as she abruptly leaned forward. 'What?'

'The case was settled,' I said, 'before the ad was put in the paper.'

'Then what in the world was the idea of putting that ad in the paper?'

'Someone wants a patsy.'

'A patsy?'

'That's right,' I said. 'They want someone who is willing to make a false affidavit for three hundred bucks.'

'Then if the case has been settled, what are they going to do with the affidavit?'

'Probably nothing.'

'I don't get you.'

'What they want is someone who is willing to commit perjury for three hundred bucks; then they'll get an affidavit in which this person swears to things that didn't exist and didn't happen and use it as a club to hold over the individual.'

'For what?'

'I don't know,' I said.

'Fry me for an oyster!' Bertha Cool said, half under her breath. 'So *that's* it!'

'I don't know,' I told her. 'I wouldn't want to report that to our client at the present time because I don't know. But what evidence I've been able to uncover seems to indicate that's the case.'

'Did they proposition you to make an affidavit, Donald?'

'Not directly. I was a little too sophisticated for them. They're looking for someone a little more shifty or a little more down on his luck.'

'And then what are they going to do?'

I made a little gesture of spreading my hands apart. 'Write your own ticket,' I told her.

Bertha's eyes glinted with enthusiasm. 'That'll be swell, Donald! I'll bet that's what Adams suspected all along, and he just wanted some confirmation. It's just like you said: he's probably representing a coalition of insurance companies who are intent upon breaking up a ring of people who are getting witnesses to commit perjury.'

'Let's not tell Adams anything until we're sure,' I said.

'Why not?'

'We don't want him to think the job was too easy.'

Bertha digested that bit of information. 'Yes, *sir*,' she said; 'I see your point.'

'Let me know if you hear from Adams,' I told her, and walked down to my office.

Elsie Brand gave me a warm smile. 'How's the case coming, Donald?'

'So-so. I want some help on it.'

She raised her eyebrows.

'Can I count on you?'

'For anything.'

'Got a very loud scarf anywhere around?'

'I . . . yes. I have an orange and red scarf.'

'Get it,' I said; 'run down to the drugstore and get yourself a pair of dark glasses, put on very vivid lipstick, and let's go.'

'Bertha won't like it if we leave your office without anyone and . . .'

'Bertha won't like it anyway,' I said. 'And there's no one else I can trust. We shouldn't be gone too long.'

'O.K.,' Elsie said.

'Let me know when you're ready,' I told her.

I looked over the morning mail. There wasn't anything particularly important. While I was studying the mail, Bertha rang the phone.

'I finally got an answer from that new number Adams left. Guess what?'

'A love nest?' I asked.

'An attorney's office – and they're very vague about Barney Adams. They asked me if I cared to state my business with Mr. Adams and leave my name.'

'So what did you do?' I asked.

Bertha said, 'I had to play things close to my chest, Donald. I said it was a personal matter and hung up.'

'Didn't leave any message – any number, any name?'

'No, I left nothing.'

'Good girl!' I told her. 'We'll probably be hearing from him later on in the day.'

I couldn't prove that there had been any connection whatever between Adams and Finchley or Harper and Finchley; and I certainly hoped there hadn't been any connection between Daphne Creston and Finchley. But I was in a delicate position.

Elsie came back with the dark glasses, put on the scarf and the lipstick, and looked a knockout.

I put her in the agency car and drove around to the

Travertine Hotel, parked in front of the place, and tapped the horn.

A bellboy came out.

'You've got some baggage you're holding for Daphne Creston,' I said. 'We'll take it now.'

He gave Elsie a quick look; then his eyes shifted to the two dollar bills I was holding.

'We're in a hurry,' I told him. 'Have to catch a plane. Make it snappy, will you?'

'It's under the name of Daphne Creston?'

'That's right,' I said, and then looked at Elsie. 'It is under your name, isn't it?'

Elsie nodded.

The bellboy entered the hotel and, within a matter of minutes, came out with the suitcase and the overnight bag.

'Don't you have a claim check on these?' he asked

'They were just put under the name of Daphne Creston,' I said. 'Load them right in the back, if you will.'

He said, 'There's supposed to be a check.'

'Forget it,' I told him. 'We're in a hurry, and those are the right things, so let's skip the red tape.'

'That's all of it?' he asked.

'That's all of it,' I told him, and jumped in behind the wheel.

By the time he had the bags loaded, I was driving away. I didn't think he bothered to check the license number.

'Now what?' Elsie asked.

'Off with the scarf,' I said. 'Off with the dark glasses; subdue the lipstick; back to the office and ride herd on what's happening.'

I dropped Elsie at the office and said, 'Don't tell anybody when I'll be in, because it's indefinite. Say I'll be in and out all day; take messages; I'll be in touch with you.'

I drove to the bus depot, put the baggage in a locker, and took stock of the situation.

Daphne Creston was somewhere in the city, penniless. I

had eliminated her back trail by picking up her baggage. She just might be mixed up in a murder case. A man by the name of Rodney Harper had a false affidavit signed and sworn to by Daphne.

The kid could be in a pack of trouble.

I decided to take a look at my new apartment, drove there, parked the car, and went in.

The curtains were pulled, the place was dark. I switched on the lights and noticed what seemed like a long bundle on the davenport.

I took another, closer look and could see a few wisps of hair straggling out from under the blanket.

A tousled head came up, frightened eyes blinked at me, and then there was a smile as Daphne said, 'Hi, Donald. You're getting in pretty late.'

'Hi, yourself,' I said. 'What's cooking?'

She said, 'I had to accept your hospitality, Donald. I didn't have a dime. I didn't have a place to stay. I left the bed for you. There was an extra blanket in the closet and I rolled up in it. I hope you don't mind.'

'What happened?' I asked.

'Donald,' she said, 'it was the craziest thing, and I guess I'm in trouble.'

'I have an idea you are.'

She said, 'I closed the windows and left the heat on last night. And it was cold about three o'clock this morning. They turned the heat off then.'

I said, 'You should have got into the bed and used the extra blanket on the bed if you got cold.'

'I didn't want to usurp your domain, Donald. If you had come home about three o'clock this morning, however, I'd have been strongly tempted. A cold girl can be very easily persuaded. Where were you? I've got no right to ask, but – Donald, there *is* somebody, isn't there?'

'Well,' I said thoughtfully, 'I didn't sleep here. That much is obvious. But what I'm interested in is what happened to you.'

She said, 'I went to the Monadnock Building. That man was there.'

'You mean Harper?'

'Yes.'

'And what did he do?'

'He had a big automobile. I think it was a Lincoln. He was impatient; he told me to get in, and we drove rapidly out past Hollywood. Then he suddenly made a left-hand turn and then he made another left-hand turn, then a right-hand turn, and then turned back toward the boulevard again and drove in at a home. I think no one was there. The house was dark. It was in the seventeen-hundred block on Hemmet Avenue.'

'What side of the street?'

'The north side.'

'Did he go in?'

'No. We just sat there in the car.'

'Where was the car?'

'Parked way back in the driveway.'

'Then what?'

'Then after ten minutes or so we went on down to this house.'

'The Finchley house?'

'I think it was.'

'Then what?'

'He said, "Now, you're supposed to go in there. Take this key and use it to open the front door. As soon as you've opened the front door, walk quietly up the stairs. There will be a small table at the head of the stairs, just to the right. Pick up the brief case which is there on the table. Go back down the stairs, out the front door, and walk to the curb. Turn either to the right or to the left – whichever you choose. Keep walking. Don't stop for anything or anybody. If anybody is following you, pretend you don't see them. Keep on walking, I'll be cruising somewhere in the neighborhood, sizing up the situation. When I make sure you aren't being followed, I'll slide in the curb, call to you and tell you to get in. Then I'll drive you back to the city. You'll be given the three hundred dollars and your job will be finished." '

'That all?' I asked.

'That's about it. Of course, he said a few things by way of explanation. He said, "I can't pay you the three hundred dollars the way things are now. As long as there's this question of your good faith and whether you actually saw the accident, my hands are tied!"

'Then he went on to say that that was what came of doing business with a lawyer who is just too darned ethical.'

'All right,' I said, 'what happened? You went in the house?'

'I used the key and opened the door. I felt misgivings, but I started upstairs and heard two people having a terrific argument. All I heard was the man. He was shouting epithets and was terribly angry.'

'Could you tell what the man was talking about?'

'No, I could only make out a word here and there, such as "traitor" and "crook" and something about betraying a confidence, and I think he said, "I've changed my mind. I'm calling your bluff." And then, all of a sudden, there was the sound of this shot. Only I didn't realize what it was at the time. I thought it was somebody slamming a door real hard; but as soon as I heard that sound, things became silent except for someone running down what sounded like back stairs.'

'What did you do?'

'I ducked into a little closet at the foot of the stairs, a cloak closet, and closed the door almost all the way.'

'And then what?'

'Then I heard this person run out of the back door and I opened the closet door. I went up the stairs. When I got far enough up to see the upper hallway, I could look through an open door and into a lighted room. I saw the table with the brief case. Only there were two brief cases. I didn't know which one to take. I decided to take the top one. Then was when I peeked into the lighted room. I saw a man's feet. I took a couple of more steps so I could get a better view. A man was sprawled out on the floor.

'It was then I realized that what I had heard must have been a shot. I was petrified.'

'So what did you do?'

'I think I screamed at least once. I know I turned and ran through a corridor and out of the house. It wasn't until after I got out I realized I was still carrying the brief case.'

'Then what?' I asked.

She said, 'I went out and stood by the front of the house looking to see if the automobile was going to come back for me. I waited two or three minutes in the deep shadows for Mr. Harper to come by, but, of course, he didn't show up. He had told me he would be cruising in the neighbourhood. I would have been reassured if I could have seen him go by, but there wasn't any car, so I moved into the shadows and stayed there, shaking like a leaf.

'Then I heard two people out on the porch of the adjoining house, and one of them said, "Did you think that could have been a pistol shot we heard?" And the other one said, "I guess it could have been. I'm going to call the police right now." '

'Just where were you standing?' I asked.

'Under an orange tree on the front lawn. That is, I think it was an orange tree. It was very dark and the foliage was quite thick.'

'Then what?'

'The people next door went inside to telephone the police, and I lost my head. Mr. Harper had said that if I would walk down the street, he would make certain that I wasn't being followed and then would cruise by and pick me up. So I ran out to the sidewalk, looked up and down the street, didn't see any headlights, and started walking; and as I walked I began to get frightened. I guess I had covered about a hundred yards when I came to a house which looked deserted. It was all dark and I guess the people were out for the evening someplace. Anyway, I felt I should get off the street, so I walked around to the back of that house and sat on the steps of the back porch for quite a while – it must have been half an hour. I heard police cars and the sounds of sirens and I was good and frightened.'

'Then what?'

'Then I got into circulation again. I was afraid to stay there too long for fear the people who owned the house would come home. So I walked and walked and walked and came to a side street that I took back to the boulevard, and there was a bench and a bus stop there. I didn't know how often buses were running at that time of the night, but I just went over and sat down. Remember that I had only about thirty-five cents to my name.'

'And then?' I asked.

'Well, a couple of cars stopped and people tried to get me to ride with them, but they were the flashy kind and it was easy to see what they were after. But a rather elderly gentleman stopped his car and seemed very nice. He said, "I beg your pardon, if you're waiting for a bus, it's going to be quite a while before one comes along. I'm going back to Hollywood and then down to Los Angeles. If I can be of any assistance, I'd be glad to have you ride with me." '

'What did you do?'

'I was getting a little cold and nervous and – well, I accepted.'

'Have any trouble?'

'Not a bit. The man was just wonderful.'

'Did he,' I asked, 'take you here?'

'No,' she said, 'I gave him an address a couple of blocks down the street. He dropped me off there and wanted to see me up to my apartment to make sure that I was all right. But I laughed at him and told him I came home late at night lots of times and there was nothing to worry about. So I ran up the steps to an apartment house, stood there at the door for a moment, then turned the knob and pushed on the door. It was open and I went in. There was no one in the lobby; I waited there for about a minute and then came back out. My nice man had driven away. So then I walked back here to your place. I knocked on your door and got no answer. I used my key and came in. I decided I was going to *have* to take advantage of your hospitality; but I didn't want to – well, you know. I didn't want to seem to – to be in *your* bed when you came in, so I looked around and found this extra blanket in the closet and took my clothes, put on a pair of pajamas and rolled up in the blanket.

'Donald, I must be a mess; I haven't a comb, hairbrush, toothbrush, no creams – I haven't anything. I'm just a forlorn waif and I must look like the tragic end of a misspent life!'

'Where is the brief case?' I asked.

'Under the couch,' she said.

She swung back the blanket.

The action was perfectly natural; there was no coyness about it, no self-consciousness; she just flung back the blanket and sat up. She was wearing a pair of my pajamas. The top two buttons were open. She bent over to reach under the couch and dragged out the brief case. The pajamas stretched tight around her hips.

'There it is, Donald,' she said, sitting up on the davenport.

It was an expensive brief case. There were no initials on it, no sign that it had ever been used. It looked brand new.

I tried the catch. It was locked.

She laughed and said, 'I did that last night, Donald. I wanted to see what was in it.'

I said, 'Just a minute,' and walked over to my own brief case, where I kept a small piece of stiff wire, which properly used is about as efficient a lock pick as anyone could ask for.

It took me less than a minute to get the brief case open.

It was full of money.

I heard Daphne say, 'Good heavens, Donald! It's . . . it's . . .' Her voice trailed away into startled silence.

I pulled out the money and said, 'We're going to have to count this so we can both be protected, Daphne.'

She nodded, spread the blanket out over her knees, and I dumped the packages of currency on to the blanket.

There was an even forty thousand dollars in the brief case.

I put it back, closed the brief case, and slid it under the couch.

'Now what do we do?' she asked.

'Now we have to try to beat the police to the punch,' I said. 'We've got to find out where we stand before they find you.'

'Donald, it *was* a pistol shot I heard, wasn't it?'

'It was a pistol shot,' I said, 'and the man who lived in that house – an attorney named Dale Finchley – is very dead. It shouldn't need any great stretch of the imagination to tell you that you're in something of a spot.'

'Donald, could I – could I take my three hundred dollars out of that brief case and . . .'

'You don't touch a cent!' I said.

'But, Donald, I can't – I'm absolutely broke and I've *got* to get out of here and get where the police can't find me.'

'You've done some fool things in the last few days,' I said, 'but running away right at the present time would be the worst mistake you could possibly make. In California, flight is an evidence of guilt. You've already resorted to flight once.'

'When?'

'When you ran from the house. You should have waited and told the police your story.'

'They wouldn't have believed me.'

'They might not have disbelieved you,' I said. 'You could have cited certain facts by way of corroboration. I could have vouched for part of your story.'

'You could?'

'Yes.'

'How?'

I said, 'I was driving the car that was following Harper when you left the Monadnock Building.'

'You were?'

'That's right.'

'Good heavens, why?'

'I wanted to find out what was up and wanted to give you some measure of protection if possible. I had an idea you might be headed for trouble.

'Why, Donald? How did you know?'

'Figure it out for yourself,' I said. 'This man Harper didn't want any affidavit to straighten out an automobile accident; he was looking for someone he could use as a patsy. He wanted someone who would be willing to execute a false affidavit. Once he had that false affidavit, he had that person in his power. He could show perjury had been committed.

'I showed up and he didn't like my looks; I was a little bit too sure of myself – perhaps a little too sophisticated. However, he would have done business with me if he had had to.

'Then you came along and you were just exactly what he was looking for – a young woman who didn't know her way around ...'

'Donald, I do know my way around. I've – I've had *lots* of experience!'

'Sure,' I said, 'you've got a certain veneer of sophistication, but you're still naïve.'

For a moment she seemed disposed to argue the point; then she settled back on the davenport, pulled up the blanket around her chin, smiled at me, and said, 'All right, Donald, I guess it's up to you to complete my education.'

'If what I think is correct,' I said, 'you're already enrolled for a postgraduate course. The police will be looking for you before midafternoon, and by tonight you'll probably be charged with murder.'

Her eyes popped wide open. 'Donald!' she exclaimed. And then after a moment she said, 'Are you kidding? Are you trying to get a rise out of me?'

'I'm telling the truth,' I told her. 'I don't know whether they had it all set up or whether you blundered into something; but you can see the sketch. You show up there at the house and ...'

'But, Donald, I never knew the man! I never saw him in my life!'

'That's your story,' I said. 'Let's look at it from the police standpoint. Finchley was murdered; he was having an argument with a woman before his murder. It could have been a woman who was trying to get blackmail. Finchley might not have wanted to have paid the blackmail.

'The woman pulled a gun and shot him. Police think this woman then took the money Finchley had picked up to make a final payment when he got the papers of whatever it was he was being blackmailed about.

'The police find you with the money.

'You tell a story about people giving you a key and telling you to go in the house and pick up a brief case. Why were you to do this? In order to get the three hundred dollars that the people owed you. Why did they owe you three hundred dollars? Because you had made a false affidavit in which you had committed perjury.

'You tell that story on the witness stand. The District Attorney takes you on cross-examination; he jeers at you, "So you were willing to commit perjury for three hundred dollars!" You tell him you were broke and hungry; and you argue and try to evade the point; but the District Attorney keeps putting it up to you. Finally you admit you were willing to commit perjury for three hundred dollars.

'The District Attorney sneers, turns his back and walks away.

'The jury takes a good, long look at you – a girl who would commit perjury for three hundred dollars. What would you do for forty thousand dollars?'

'Donald, stop it!' she said.

'Life isn't like that,' I told her. 'It isn't like a television show that you can turn off by twisting a dial. It isn't like a motion-picture machine where you can shut off the flickering images at any time you like.

'Life goes forward – a steady, remorseless procession of cause and effect. Today's effects becomes tomorrow's causes.

Once you start a chain of events, it's hard to break the sequence.

'Now you take a bath and get dressed. I'm going down and get your baggage.'

'It's up at the hotel,' she said. 'I'll stay up there and ... Will they be looking for me, Donald?'

'Of course they'll be looking for you,' I told her.

'And if they find you before we have more facts in our possession, they're going to try us for murder.'

'Us?' she asked incredulously.

'Us,' I said. 'I followed you down there. I was fooling around the place waiting to pick you up.'

'But you didn't pick me up.'

'Try and tell that to the police,' I said. 'They find you in my apartment, where you spent the night; they find *us* with the money in *our* possession.'

'Donald, they don't need to know that.'

'Yes, they do,' I told her. 'Don't underestimate the police. They know I was out there last night trying to follow a car. They'll find out all about the rest of it. Our only hope is to get enough facts together so that, when they find out about us, we can put more facts in their possession – so that we can put all our cards on the table and they'll give us a clean bill of health. I'm going to get your baggage.'

'Won't it be dangerous for you to go to the hotel?'

'I've already been to the hotel,' I told her. 'I have your baggage in a locker. I'll get it and bring it up.

'There's a dozen eggs, some bacon in the refrigerator. There's a coffeecake in that carton. And, remember, I don't like a ring in the bathtub.'

CHAPTER FIVE

I CAME back with the baggage. The aroma of coffee and broiling bacon greeted me as I opened the door.

Daphne had the place all tidied up, the blanket folded and put away in the closet, the bathroom a little steamy but spotlessly clean. She took the coffeecake out of the oven, dumped eggs from a bowl into a frying pan.

'Straight up, over easy, or scrambled?' she asked.

'How do you like them?'

'All three ways, but you're the man of the house.'

'Scrambled soft,' I told her.

'Scrambled soft it is,' she said; and a couple of minutes later gave me a hot plate with scrambled eggs, broiled bacon and coffeecake, with a cup of fragrant coffee.

It was good coffee, the eggs were perfect, and the bacon was broiled just the way I like it.

She was watching me anxiously. 'How am I doing, Donald?'

'So far, O.K.'

'Well, that's a good beginning,' she said. 'Let's hope I can go the distance – and give satisfaction. What do I do next?'

'You stay here,' I said. 'Cook yourself some lunch. If anybody wants to know who you are, you're Mrs. Lam. There are enough groceries here for lunch and lots of canned goods. I'll be back with some fresh meat in time for dinner. Stay right here. There's a television that works. You'll have to kill time. Don't go out under any circumstances; don't fraternize with any of the people in the adjoining apartments.'

'But, Donald, if they're looking for me and I'm going under the name of Mrs. Lam . . .'

I said, 'Sergeant Sellers would forgive me for living in sin. He wouldn't forgive me for concealing a witness. He'd *never* forgive me for whisking a suspect out from under his nose.'

'Donald, what are we going to do with that brief case with all the money?'

'We're going to leave it here,' I said.

'Is it safe?'

'Of course it isn't safe. It isn't safe anywhere.'

'Couldn't you go to a bank and . . .'

'And what?' I asked. 'Let the bank records show that we got a safety-deposit box and put this hot money in it? There's only one safe place for that money, and that's in the hands of the police. But the minute I let the police know we have it, the fat's in the fire. Take care of yourself; I'll be seeing you later.'

I walked out and left her looking woebegone and frightened.

As a modern detective agency, we had quite a few mechanical aids to assist us in our work – electric spotting devices by which we could fasten a little gadget to a car we wanted to follow and follow it by a series of beep signals. We also had a new device, a telespotter.

The telespotter is about the size of a small radio, actuated by batteries and transistors. Within a reasonable distance of a telephone, the telespotter will give the number that is being dialed on the telephone.

Electronic impulses actuate the mechanism and start a roll of thin paper being unwound. That paper consists of a string of numbers – 1, 2, 3, 4, 5, 6, 7, 8, 9, 0. As the telephone which is being monitored starts dialing, the paper starts unwinding. As soon as the dial of any single number is completed, the numbers are punched out on the telespotter, the paper zips out to a point just past the zero, and the mechanism starts in all over again for the next number.

I went to my apartment, picked up a brief case, made sure the telespotter was in perfect working order, and slipped it in the brief case.

I drove to the Monadnock Building and went up to 1624.

The same woman sat at the desk. This time there were several people waiting.

'You had an ad,' I said, 'about witnesses . . .'

'Oh, yes. However, I'm sorry, the witnesses who were needed have been found and . . . Say, weren't you one of the . . . Why, yes, you came in here and . . .'

'That's right,' I said. 'I talked with Mr. Harper, and I want to see him again.'

She shook her head. 'I'm afraid that's impossible. Mr. Harper isn't available.'

'Can you take a message for him?'

'I'm not certain that I'll see Mr. Harper for – well, for some time. He comes and goes. However, I can try to get a message to him.'

I said, 'When you get in touch with him, tell him that perjury is a felony.'

'Oh, I'm quite sure he knows that,' she said.

'And,' I went on, 'tell him that suborning perjury consists of soliciting another person to commit perjury. That is an offense that is punishable by imprisonment in a state prison. Tell him that on that April fifteenth accident the Cadillac was the one that went through the signal and was at fault – and that the case had been settled long before he put his ad in the paper. Ask him what he intends to do next.'

She was looking at me with wide, startled eyes. 'The accident was settled *before* the ad was put in the paper?'

'Right.'

'How do you know?'

'I made it my business to find out.'

'How '

'I talked with the parties.'

'Well, of all the crazy things!' she said.

I said nothing, stood there letting the idea soak in.

'But what is there *I* can do?' she asked.

I said, 'Mr. Harper is a client of yours. He might feel that you are entitled to an explanation.'

'And then?'

'And then you might pass the explanation on to me.'

'You feel that you're entitled to an explanation?'

'Certainly. I answered the ad. I went to considerable time and trouble.'

'Oh, I see. You feel that you're entitled to compensation?'

'Definitely not,' I said. 'I'm not coming here for money; I'm not coming here with my hand out. I'm coming here for an explanation. That's what I'd like to have – and that's what I'm going to get, sooner or later, one way or another.'

'Well, it *is* rather puzzling, isn't it?' she said, giving me the best she could conjure up in the way of a dazzling smile. 'I'll try and get in touch with Mr. Harper – although his arrangement with me was on a temporary basis and I'm not sure I can reach him at the moment. Your interest is only that of . . .'

'Of getting a clear explanation of what happened,' I said. 'I would like to be sure that no crime was committed.'

'No crime?'

'An attempt to suborn perjury.'

'I see.'

'It would be very inconvenient for me to report a crime as having been committed if it turns out there was a reasonable, logical explanation for everything that had been done.'

'Yes,' she said acidly, 'in dealing with reputable business people, an erroneous report of that nature could prove very embarrassing – very embarrassing indeed.'

'All right,' I said; 'you understand my position. I want to be fair but I also want an explanation.'

'It seems to me you've put in a lot of time on this thing simply because you answered an ad.'

I smiled at her and said, 'That's right. I've put in a *lot* of time on it, and I don't want to have to put in more with the Better Business Bureau.'

'I see,' she said dubiously. 'Now, where can I get in touch with you, Mr. Lam?'

I said, 'In all probability I had better be the one who gets in touch with you because I am in and out and . . .'

'But surely you have some address.'

'I have an address,' I told her, 'but I keep moving around. I'd better keep in touch with you rather than have you try to get in touch with me.'

I gave her my best smile and walked out.

As soon as the door closed behind me, I walked a few steps so I was approximately opposite the receptionist's desk, opened my brief case, and took out my telespotter and turned on the switch.

For a moment, nothing happened; but then, suddenly, the transistor-actuated machinery started reeling out a strip of paper.

I got the phone number, 676-2211

I folded the strip of paper, replaced the telespotter and walked to the elevator.

I called my office and got Elsie Brand on the telephone.

'Elsie,' I said, 'you've got to do a job for me. Jump in a cab, come to the Monadnock Building at once. Bring your notebook. I'll meet you there. You'll be on a job for perhaps two or three hours. If you have any good walking shoes in the office, put them on. You're going to have to do a shadowing job for me.'

She said, 'Donald, you know Bertha doesn't like that. She doesn't like to have me go out . . .'

'This is an emergency,' I told her. 'I haven't time to get any other person. Get over here just as fast as you can.'

'I'll be there right away, Donald,' she promised.

I hung up and waited around the entrance of the building until Elsie arrived.

I paid off her cab, then took her into a little lunch counter and coffee stand in the lobby of the building.

'You've got to get this right,' I told her, 'and it's going to be difficult. Sit here and watch the elevators. They'll be busy and crowded during the lunch hour, but there aren't enough elevators so you can't keep an eye on the people who come out.

'Now, then, the person I want is about thirty-two years old; she's a woman five feet four inches tall, weighing one hundred and twenty pounds. That doesn't mean anything; you've got to watch for her clothes. She has on a dark-blue plaid outfit with red collar and cuffs on the jacket, and there's a little bunch of red flowers at her throat.

'When that woman comes out, I want you to follow her. I want to find out where she goes; and if she talks with anyone, I want you to find out who that person is, if possible. In order to do that, you've got to shadow the person she talks with until he or she gets in an automobile. Pick up the license number of the automobile.

'I want you to take down a complete description of the person or persons she talks with – how they're dressed, the color of their hair – everything you can find out.

'You'll need expense money. Here's fifty-five dollars. You may have to run up a cab bill.

'Sit here at the lunch counter drinking coffee and toying with a piece of pie until you feel you may have begun to attract attention. Then get two cabs. Have them parked at the curb on opposite sides of the street. Put them on waiting time. Sit in one of the cabs and wait.'

'Wouldn't it be better to get just one cab and have it in readiness . . .'

'No,' I said, 'she'll come out of the lobby. If she turns down the street, your cab will be headed in the wrong direction. You can't make a U-turn within a matter of blocks. You'd have to go around the block to pick her up, and that's probably going to be too dangerous. So you have a cab on the other side all ready and waiting.'

'When will I have an opportunity to report?'

'I don't know. Find out whom she talks with, then go back to the office and wait. I'll get in touch with you sometime during the afternoon.'

'There's one other thing. If this woman uses a telephone booth, pretend that you're waiting for her to complete her call. Stand looking over her shoulder and try to get the number that she calls.

'Now, don't get too worked up about this, Elsie. I want the information very much indeed, but I realize what a difficult job I'm giving you; and if she gets away without you spotting her, that's all there'll be to it. We're taking a gamble, that's all.

'She's running a business office and she'll be staying up there until it's time for lunch. But I think she'll go out for lunch.'

'Do you know if she always does?'

'She doesn't do it always,' I said. 'If she has an emergency, she rents one of the offices during the noon hour. But I think she only does that in an emergency. However, we can't tell.'

'What office is she in, Donald?'

'Sixteen twenty-four,' I said. 'She runs an answering service and office rentals. Do the best you can. If we don't pick her up at noon, we'll have to try something else and shadow her when she gets off at night. That's going to be a lot more difficult.'

'I'll do the best I can, Donald,' she promised.

'Good enough,' I told her.

I left the building, went to a phone booth, dialed 676-2211. A beautifully modulated voice said, 'Lathrop, Lucas and Manly.'

I said, 'Wrong number; sorry,' and hung up.

CHAPTER SIX

I MADE it a point to keep away from the office and from all of my accustomed haunts. I had coffee and ice cream in a little French restaurant where most of the patrons were regular and where they didn't try to hurry anyone through the meal.

I bought the early edition of the afternoon paper and read everything I could find about the murder of Dale Finchley.

Finchley was a distinguished member of the Bar, but his practice was largely political. He was seldom seen in court; in fact, he was known as a man who kept his clients out of court, and most of his clients were the sort of men who would pay big money to be kept out of trouble.

Finchley had a palatial house in which he lived by himself, having servants come in by the day. He was a widower and something of a recluse, although he frequented a couple of exclusive clubs. Wealthy, socially acceptable, entirely unencumbered, affable, polished, magnetic – he was much sought after.

The man was an avid reader and maintained a library in his house which was well stocked with books. In this room, old-fashioned, overstuffed leather chairs and comfortable reading lights gave Finchley a chance to spend many of his evenings in quiet relaxation.

Friends stated that the lawyer had expensive radio and television sets; that he listened to news, to certain commentators, and to the weather. But, aside from that, he had little use for those channels of amusement which had so changed the reading habits of the nation.

He had a study in his house on the second floor where he transacted much of his business. And it was rumored that many of his clients preferred to drop in at night and discuss their problems in the big old-fashioned library downstairs rather than be seen going to Finchley's office by daylight.

At the time of his death, Finchley had evidently been having a quarrel with someone who had aroused his anger. It was not known whether this person was a man or a woman. It was known that Finchley had been shot once with a .38 caliber revolver; but the murderer had evidently taken the gun away with him, as police found no trace of the weapon.

It was thought that perhaps Finchley had been preparing to go out, because there was a brief case on a table at the head of the staircase which contained a summary of bids which were being submitted on a grading, road-development and storm-drainage project in a sub-division, for which Finchley acted as attorney.

These were not sealed bids but were in a file marked 'Highly Confidential' and were not supposed to be given out until the contract was awarded.

Because of the position of the brief case and the contents, police felt that Finchley had intended to see some member or members of the subdivision project that night. But each of the members stated that, while he would not have been surprised if Finchley had called him to ask for an appointment, he had had no communication from him on the evening of his death.

However, police felt the only explanation for the brief case's being on that little table at the head of the stairs was that Finchley was either intending to go out and take the data with him or was planning to go to the library on the lower floor and discuss details with some member of the commission. Police intimated that they would appreciate it if all members of the commission would submit a schedule of where they had been during the evening, and particularly at what hours they had been absent from their homes.

Police *said* they wanted these schedules to check and see if Finchley might have been trying to get in touch with some one of the members but had been unable to reach him.

Orville Maxton, one of the commissioners, resented this request by the police. 'It is too much like asking us to furnish an alibi,' he is reported to have snapped. 'I'll be damned if I do it!'

Police had learned that Finchley was inclined to keep large sums of cash in the house. His safe was opened in the presence of a state inheritance tax appraiser and was found to contain some one hundred and fifty thousand dollars in cash. There had, however, never been the slightest suspicion that Finchley was putting away money in the form of cash in order to avoid paying an income tax, because he deposited his earnings, then withdrew large sums of cash.

It was generally understood that Finchley had been dealing with one or more lobbyists whose identities were unknown. These lobbysists were known for receiving large sums of money for which they made no accounting except to 'get results'. Presumably the money went to political candidates for 'campaign expenses'.

Finchley had, from time to time, told associates that he himself made substantial contributions to the campaign expenses of various prominent public figures. And it was known that many of the political giants in the state sought Finchley's advice from time to time.

Police had recovered the fatal bullet and announced that it had been fired from a .38-caliber Colt revolver.

Had the weapon been a so-called automatic, the ejected empty cartridge case would have been found in the study. No such cartridge case was found. There had been but one shot fired, according to the testimony of the neighbors who had heard Finchley's voice raised in anger, quite evidently having a quarrel with some individual.

Because one of the neighbors had distinctly heard a woman

scream, it was thought that perhaps a woman had wielded the fatal gun.

The newspaper painted a somewhat cautious picture of a middle-aged, honored member of the Bar: the confidant of important political figures in state and city politics; a big, dignified individual who had, at the time of his death, been jarred from the even equanimity which usually characterized him – had lost his temper and had shouted curses.

I read the newspaper account twice in order to see if there was anything I had missed.

How did the person who hired Daphne know that that brief case would be on the table at the head of the stairs? It seemed possible that Finchley had told him so. It was also quite possible that when Finchley had an appointment to discuss business matters with someone in the library he would collect the data from his office, bring it home and put it there on the little table, where it would be available, either from his study or in going down for a consultation in the library. It was also possible Harper knew of this custom.

Under those circumstances, what about Daphne?

Had she been used in a daring scheme to get those documents? And perhaps had picked up the wrong brief case? Or did she pick up the right brief case?

There was one possible explanation.

It was mentioned in the newspaper that the nature of the improvements covered in the bids consisted of a package running generally in the eight-hundred-thousand-dollar figure.

It was quite possible that the brief case containing forty thousand dollars was a so-called 'good faith' deposit on the amount of an eight-hundred-thousand-dollar bid which had just been made and the deposit accepted.

Daphne's false affidavit not only placed her in the power of the people who were running the conspiracy but made it so that, if she had ever repented of the part she had played and took the stand to tell her story, her testimony would be promptly discredited by showing that she was willing to commit perjury for hire.

I finished my light lunch and again called the second number Adams had given us. The girl who answered the telephone told me that Mr. Adams had not been in, that he was keeping an important luncheon engagement; said if I would leave my name she would give Mr. Adams any message I cared to transmit, but she thought it might be late in the afternoon before he came in.

I said, 'All right, I'll leave a message for him. Tell him it's about an ad in the paper. Tell him I've been trying to get in touch with him.'

'What's the name?' she asked.

'Adams,' I said.

'No, no. *Your* name.'

'Tell him it's Mr. Trubel calling – T-R-U-B-E-L.'

'Very well, I'll tell him '

I said, 'You might also tell him there are several ways of spelling my name,' and hung up the phone.

CHAPTER SEVEN

I WENT to the office. Bertha wasn't back from lunch. I walked across the reception room into my own private office and waited for Elsie.

Bertha came in after about five minutes. I waited a minute for her to get settled, then went in to see her.

'Donald,' she said, 'I wish there was some way we could get in touch with our client.'

'You mean Adams?'

'I've called him twice. I've also left a message for him.'

'I've called him twice. I've also left a message for him.'

'Yesterday he was so anxious to talk with you. You know, Donald, I think that guy is trying to get us to forget the whole business, get what money back he can, and let it all go.'

'Could be,' I said.

'Are you pigeonholing the case?'

'No, I'm keeping on the job.'

'How're you doing?'

'I'm making a little progress. It's slow but – there's no use bothering *you* with a lot of details. I'll report to Adams when I get in touch with him. But I can't *keep* calling him.

'If the guy's trying to call off the job, let him get in touch with us and tell us what he wants.'

'That's good logic,' Bertha said. 'I get sore at these god-damned clients that can't make up their own minds. First they blow hot; then they blow cold. Somehow this guy didn't impress me like that. I thought he was a keen, incisive businessman.

'You could tell, though, he was keeping something back. At the time, I thought you were right that several insurance companies had banded together in order to get information about some sort of a racket that was jeopardizing their interests.'

I stretched, yawned and said, 'If he rings up and asks for me, tell him I'm out.'

'I'll let Elsie do the talking.'

'Elsie isn't here.'

'The hell she isn't!'

'She's out doing a tailing job for me.'

'Donald, you can't use that girl as an operative. She's a secretary. You'll get into trouble trying to . . .'

'I know, I know,' I said. 'This is an emergency.'

'I don't like it, Donald. You have too damn many emergencies. Keep this one to a minimum.'

'O.K., Bertha,' I said, and walked out.

I went down to my office and hadn't been there over ten minutes when Elsie came in.

Elsie was walking on air. The starry-eyed look on her face indicated that she had been highly successful. If she had followed her own inclination, she'd have come close to me and said, 'Donald, guess what?' As it was, however, she was playing the part of the cool operative.

'Get anywhere, Elsie?' I asked, knowing that my remark was what she was waiting for.

'Donald,' she said, 'you'd never guess . . .'

'Yes. What happened?'

'I picked up the girl from your description. That was a wonderful description, Donald. I had no trouble picking her up from the way you described her clothes and her general appearance. She went from the elevator to the entrance of the building and stood there for a minute, with people streaming all around her. And then this man came up to her.

'The man was undoubtedly the one whom she was expecting. They acted as if they'd made a date over the telephone.'

'Can you describe him?'

'I can do better than that,' she said triumphantly. 'He was the man who came in when we were serving you the birthday cake.'

I didn't try to keep surprise out of my voice. 'Barney Adams?'

She nodded. 'That's the one.'

'Where did they go?'

'They went to a cocktail lounge, had a quick drink, did a little talking, and that's when I made the wrong decision.'

'How come?'

'The way this girl acted, it looked as if they had agreed on something – some plan of action; and I thought you'd want to know what it was, where she was going. The man got up and went to the men's room, and while he was in there this girl got up and started for the door. So I reached a quick decision and decided to tail her, because I knew that you and Bertha had the address of this Adams man.'

'And where did she go?' I asked.

'Right back to her office. Probably she had some telephoning to do.'

'And didn't have any lunch?'

'No, just a drink.'

'And she left while the man was in the men's room?'

'That's right.'

'Had he called for a check, or did he pay for the drink when it was served?'

'Neither. The waiter was hovering around the table when I left. I think he was afraid they were pulling a fast one on the check. It was the girl who paid the check. I probably should have tried to see where Adams went, but it never occurred to me the girl was just going back to her office and ... well, you see, Adams knew me by sight, and I was just afraid that he was going to find me shadowing him and–well, you know, he probably wouldn't have placed me right at the start. He'd have done a little frowning concentration at first, thinking that I had a face that was vaguely familiar, and then – well, he'd have placed me, and *then* things would have been bad. So I reached the best decision I could and tailed the girl who didn't know me. She just went back to the office, and that's that!'

'Wait for her to come out?'

'I waited long enough to make sure she hadn't forgotten something and had just gone up in the elevator to get it. I thought perhaps she was going to come back down and go back to the cocktail lounge to meet him. But she stayed up there, so I guess they had transacted their business and she took off. But it was strange she went while he was in the men's room. It didn't look as though they had said any farewells or anything.'

'Look here, had he seen you?' I asked.

'I thought of that, Donald, but I'm quite sure he hadn't. If he had, he's a genius. He let his eyes slide over my face once, but just the casual glance of a man who is appraising the scenery.'

'But he *did* see you?'

'Well, of course he saw me. I was where I could look at him; and that means that he, of course, was where he could look at me.'

'And that was before he got up and went to the men's room?'

'Yes.'

'O.K., Elsie,' I told her, 'you've done a job. Don't say anything about this to Bertha. Let her know you are back in the office and will take any calls from people who are asking for me. And tell everybody I'm out.'

From the office, I went directly to the Better Business Bureau.

I took the ad from my pocket – the one I had clipped from the newspaper – and said, 'I'd like to find out something about this.'

'The girl who was at the counter said, 'Just a minute, please. I think we can help you.'

She vanished into an inside office, and a moment later a woman I knew came out.

'Why, Donald Lam!' Evelyn Calhoun said. 'What are you doing here? Sleuthing?'

'First tell me what *you* are doing *here*?' I asked.

'I've been here for six months,' she said. 'I quit my job at the City Attorney's office in order to take this position.'

I slipped the ad back in my pocket, said, 'I didn't know you were here. Actually, I didn't have anything in particular on my mind. I wanted to find out about two or three things, but I'll get a little more data and come back.'

'Perhaps you won't need the additional data,' she said 'The receptionist tells me you were inquiring about the ad offering three hundred dollars reward for a witness to an automobile accident.'

'That was one of the things I had in mind,' I said. 'Business is sort of dull, and I'm very curious. I was just nosing around. But it's nothing to bother you with.'

She laughed and said, 'Donald, don't pull that line. I know you too well. You're trying to cover up and back out because you didn't want your real identity to be known. Come on in the inner office, Donald. I think perhaps I can help you.'

I followed her into the inner office and took the seat she offered.

'What's your interest in it, Donald?' she asked.

I shook my head. 'I would have lied to the girl out there, but I'm not going to lie to you, Evelyn. So let's just forget the whole business.'

She smiled 'I won't press you, Donald. But, as a matter of fact, we have some data on that. We made an investigation – just checking because of the peculiar way the ad was worded.

'The ad was placed by a Rodney Harper, who rented an office in the Monadnock Building from Katherine Elliott.

'Katherine Elliott is a very competent secretary and organizer who quit a salaried job as secretary and branched out on her own. She has a string of small offices in the Monadnock Building. She rents them out, runs a mail-answering service and a telephone-answering service. She had a client who got into trouble with the Better Business Bureau a couple of years ago, and she's been rather careful ever since. She wanted Rodney Harper to give her references, and finally he did so – giving her a reference from the construction firm of Lathrop, Lucas and Manly. They stated that they had known Rodney Harper for some time and could vouch for his integrity.'

'Did *you* talk with Lathrop, Lucas and Manly?' I asked.

'No,' she said. 'we didn't check any further than with Katherine Elliott. Everything seemed to be all right. And, while the ad was worded in a peculiar way and the reward was a little high, we accepted Harper's references and let it go at that.'

'Katherine Elliott had checked them?'

'Oh, yes, she got one of the partners in the firm on the telephone, and he confirmed everything that was said in the letter.'

'And she has Harper's address?'

'As I remember it, she only had a hotel address. Harper was here from another city doing some kind of investigative work in connection with the accident. But, in view of the gilt-edged nature of his references, she went ahead with Harper.'

'You didn't find out what hotel Harper was staying at, did you?'

'No, I just made a routine check. I *can* find out for you, Donald.'

'If you can find out without letting me get mixed in it in any way . . .'

'Don't give it a thought,' she said. 'I'll be glad to do it for you.'

'She pulled out a drawer full of cards, got a number, and dialed.

'Katherine Elliott, please. Oh, yes, Katherine. This is Evelyn Calhoun at the Better Business Bureau. I was trying to complete my card file on the matter I consulted you about, and I notice we don't have Mr. Harper's address. I believe you said he was at a hotel . . .'

The telephone broke into squawking noises which sounded like a panic-stricken hen gathering her chicks about her when a chicken hawk flew overhead.

'Oh, yes, I see,' Evelyn Calhoun said, when she could get a word in edgeways; and then, after a moment, 'Well, I was just completing my file and I saw, on looking at the card, that we didn't have that address. The Stilton Hotel. Well, thanks a lot . . . No, no, everything's all right. I was just completing our files. The matter is closed as far as we are concerned. . . . That's right. . . . You know how it is. You like to keep your desk clear. . . . That's right. These things certainly do pile up. I hadn't noticed that we didn't have that data until I started to file. You probably gave it to me before, but I didn't put it down. The fact he was vouched for by the contractors is enough for anyone. . . . All right, thanks again. 'Bye now!'

Evelyn Calhoun hung up the phone and said, 'My, you are an unpopular character!'

'Why?'

'She gave me the information I wanted, and then told me that a Donald Lam, who had made a pass at trying to get the reward from Mr. Harper and been turned down, was trying to make trouble.

'She said that Harper was satisfied that Donald Lam hadn't seen the accident at all but was simply trying to collect three hundred dollars and was willing to commit perjury in order to do it.

'She went on to say that, under the circumstances, they couldn't accuse Lam of trying to sell his testimony without putting themselves in a vulnerable position, so they had just kind of brushed him off, but that Lam was persistent and certainly wanted that three hundred dollars.'

'I see,' I said.

She regarded me thoughtfully. '*Did* you try to collect the three hundred dollars, Donald?'

'I tried to find out what the ad was all about.'

'Did you find anything?'

'In a way,' I said. 'It's fishy.'

'In what way?'

'I'm not prepared to make a detailed statement at the moment,' I said, 'but that accident is completely phony. They've got everything all backward in the ad. The driver of the Cadillac was the one who was at fault. The accident was settled before that ad was ever put in the paper.'

Her eyes narrowed. '*The accident was settled!*'

'That's right.'

'Then why on earth would they want to get testimony? Are they trying to reopen the settlement?'

'I don't know,' I said. 'I was just trying to get information myself.'

'I think we'd better look into that,' she said. 'This is right down our alley.'

I shook my head. 'Don't stir up the waters until after I've made a pass at catching my fish.'

'But those are the sort of things we like to catch. Well, I may as well tell you . . . Katherine Elliott was in trouble once before with one of her clients, and if she's . . . But she told us she used every precaution.'

'I'm satisfied she did,' I said. 'Just let it go for the time being. Can you give me Katherine Elliott's address?'

She consulted a card, said, 'She was living in the Steel-built Apartments in apartment 14 B. That was when she was having a little trouble with the B.B.B. I don't know if she's still at the same place.'

'I don't know as it makes much difference,' I said. 'I'm like you; I just like to have lots of data.'

'Lots of data sometimes comes in mighty handy,' she said, and then went on: 'Let's make a bargain, Donald.'

'What?'

'You tell us what you find out if it is something we should know and we'll back your play if it comes to a showdown.'

'What do you mean "back my play"?'

'Say that we're working on it together – if that will help.'

'The time may come,' I said, 'when that will help. But, right now, I want to play a lone hand. I'll co-operate with you every way that I can, but I have a client and some things I have to keep confidential.'

'I understand. But you've got me interested now.'

'Don't show any interest in the outer office.'

'O.K. Donald. Keep in touch.'

'Thanks,' I told her, and left the office to go to the public library and check up on construction firms doing business in the city.

I found a contractor's magazine and studied the files. Finally I found a reference to Lathrop, Lucas and Manly in the index.

The assistant librarian helped me find the issue I wanted, and I opened it to the page dealing with the firm.

There were pictures of the three executives.

Making allowances for the fact that the article was five years old, the picture of Walter Cushman Lucas was quite recognizable.

Walter Lucas was Rodney Harper.

CHAPTER EIGHT

The office of Lathrop, Lucas and Manly was the last word in modern decor.

The main reception room had chairs for clients who were waiting and a receptionist who sat at a desk with a switchboard at her left hand. Then there was a stenographic and filing room which opened to one side and from which came the sound of clacking typewriters.

From the main room, there were three doors, leading to private offices labelled, 'MR. LATHROP', 'MR. LUCAS', 'MR. MANLY'.

The receptionist had ability. She was all hands, arms and fingers, working the switchboard, typing cards on an electric machine which she made sound like a Gattling gun in between telephone calls.

I stood watching her for a moment, which evidently annoyed her somewhat. She kept a smile in her voice, but she couldn't keep a frown from her forehead.

'Yes?' she asked.

'Mr. Lucas,' I said.

'Oh, yes. And your name, please?'

I said, 'Tell Mr. Lucas it's a personal matter. He'll know me when he sees me.'

I smiled.

She didn't smile, but said, 'I'll have to have your name.'

'Tell him it's Donald,' I said in a bored voice.

'Donald what?' she asked.

I made a bluff of turning toward the door. 'Oh, well,' I

said, 'it's just a personal matter. When you see him again, tell him that Donald was in but didn't like the red tape. He'll know what you mean.'

'Just a moment,' she said icily.

Her fingers flew over the switchboard, pulling out a cord and depressing a key.

She turned a cold shoulder to me, lowered her voice, and spoke into the telephone in such a way that I couldn't hear what she said.

A moment later she said, 'Yes, Mr. Lucas, I'll ask him.'

She said, 'Mr. Lucas would like your name, please.'

I gave her my most cheerful smile, 'All right,' I said, 'I'll give it to him.'

I walked past her desk, turned the knob of the door marked 'MR. LUCAS,' found it was unlocked, and walked in.

Lucas was still sitting with the telephone at his ear, frowning in irritation.

He looked up with cold anger on his face, slammed the telephone down, pushed back his chair, got to his feet – and then his eyes widened in recognition, his jaw sank. I saw the aggressive set leave his shoulders. All of a sudden the coat looked too big for the man.

'You!' he said.

I closed the door.

I said, 'I have been waiting to hear from you. Naturally, I would like my three hundred dollars.'

'How . . . how did you locate me?'

I smiled. 'Does it make any difference, Mr. Lucas? Or do you prefer to be called Mr. Harper when we're discussing that automobile accident?'

He settled back in his chair, hesitated a moment, said, 'Sit down, Mr. Lam.'

I took the chair he indicated.

'I think perhaps I owe you an explanation,' he said.

'I think perhaps you do.'

He hesitated for a long time, caressing the knuckles of his

right hand with the fingers of his left hand, evidently trying to coordinate his thoughts.

'That ad,' he said, 'was perhaps misleading.'

'Perhaps.'

'We wanted to get in touch with a certain person whom we had reason to believe had seen the accident. We wanted that person for another reason altogether; but we didn't want to disclose our true reason, so my associates and I decided to advertise for persons who might have seen the automobile accident.'

'I see.'

His face brightened a little as he went along. 'So, actually, the ad could have been misleading to a bona fide witness to the accident. We didn't want that. Apparently, you were inconvenienced. We would expect to compensate you for that inconvenience.'

'How much,' I asked.

His smile was affable now. 'A hundred dollars, Mr. Lam.'

'The ad said three hundred,' I said.

'I have explained to you, Mr. Lam, that the ad was directed toward a very special person, and you are *not* that person.'

'Did you find the person you wanted?' I asked.

He said, 'I think that's hardly pertinent to the subject we're discussing, Mr. Lam.'

'What subject were we discussing?'

'Your compensation,' he said, and then added after a moment, 'if any.'

I said, 'For your information, that ad was a complete fabrication. You must have had your ideas completely mixed. Actually, it was the Cadillac that ran the red light. The Ford Galaxie was running with the traffic, according to the signal.'

'That wasn't the way you talked when I first discussed the matter,' he said.

'That's the way I'm talking now – the way the facts are.'

'Then you didn't see the accident?' he said.

'The ad offered a three-hundred-dollar reward to someone who could furnish a witness who *had* seen the accident.'

'The ad was very carefully worded,' Lucas said, 'so that the reward was only to be paid to a witness who would testify that the driver of the Ford was in the wrong.'

I said, 'Yes, you couldn't afford to have had the ad otherwise because you'd have had perhaps as many as half-a-dozen witnesses.'

'Exactly what is it you want?' he asked.

I said, 'I think I'm entitled to the three hundred dollars. I answered the ad in good faith, didn't I?'

'I don't know,' he said. 'Did you.'

I simply smiled.

He hesitated, ran his fingers along the angle of his chin, then doubled up his left fist and rubbed the tips of the right fingers over the knuckles. Finally, he said, 'Very well, Mr. Lam. Perhaps you're entitled to the reward after all. You'll have to pardon me for a moment, because I don't keep this kind of money in my pocket. I'll have to draw a voucher and then get the cash from the safe. It will take a few minutes. If you'll just wait here.'

He got up and left the office.

I was tempted to get up and look around on his desk, but a mirror in the wall looked very much like one of those one-way windows to me, and so I sat there waiting.

After about five minutes, he was back with three one-hundred-dollar bills and a receipt.

'Here you are, Mr. Lam,' he said.

He handed me the three one-hundred-dollar bills and said, 'You sign here on the receipt.'

The receipt read, 'I, Donald Lam, acknowledge receipt in full payment of compensation due to me for answering an ad and locating witnesses for traffic accident dated April 15, as the ad appeared in the daily papers.'

There was a blank for signature and, below the blank, two lines for address.

'You'll have to sign your name,' Lucas said, 'and be sure to give us the address.'

I folded the three one-hundred dollar bills, put them in my pocket, took the form of receipt in my fingers, tore it in two, then tore the two halves in two, walked over and dropped them into the wastebasket.

'No receipt,' I said, and walked out.

He sat there looking at me, frustrated, angry and undecided.

As I left the office, a good-looking girl who had been seated in one of the chairs said to the receptionist, 'I can't wait any longer. Please tell him I'll try and see him tomorrow. I have an appointment.'

She preceded me out of the door.

We waited together for the elevator.

I sized her up as an exceptionally clever stenographer who had been given the job of tailing me to see where I went. She was thrilled to death at getting away from her routine work and having a job of shadowing.

The elevator cage came to a stop and the girl walked in ahead of me, giving herself away with almost every move she made.

The technique of shadowing is an art, and it isn't easy to learn. This girl was doing everything wrong.

She was nervous; she cleared her throat three or four times while the elevator was descending; she carefully avoided turning her face toward mine, but she would make little surreptitious, sidelong glances of appraisal, as though afraid I might vanish into thin air while the elevator was in motion.

When we reached the street, she let me get out first – despite the fact I held back.

There was a cocktail lounge a couple of blocks down the street. I walked directly there, as though expecting to meet someone.

She waited until I had entered and had a chance to look all around, putting on the act of looking for someone who was to have met me, before she came in and took a seat – very prim, very dignified, very self-contained, hoping that I wouldn't recognize her as the girl who had been in the elevator and the girl who had been in the contractor's office.

Even so, she couldn't refrain from those little nervous, sidelong glances.

I talked with the bartender, asking him what time it was. We compared our watches. I went into the men's room. There was an entrance from the bar and from the big dining room.

I walked in through the bar entrance and walked out through the door to the dining room, hit the street and kept going.

I found an unpretentious hotel, went in and registered as 'Donald Lam of Denver, Colorado.' I explained to the clerk that I had left my baggage at the depot in a locker, that it would be out directly, but that, since I had no baggage, I'd pay in advance.

He welcomed the suggestion.

I paid for the room for one night, got a receipt, got my key, thrust it in my pocket and said, 'I won't go up to the room just yet but will wait for my baggage.'

I walked out, then went directly back to the building where Lathrop, Lucas and Manly had their offices.

I waited around the entrance to the building for nearly twenty minutes before she showed up.

She was looking dispirited and dejected as she came walking along the sidewalk.

I walked out and went past her, apparently without seeing her but with my eyes straight ahead. I could still see the sudden start of surprise on her face as she recognized me in the crowd. I saw her twist her neck, then her body, then follow me.

I led her directly to the hotel, walked up to the desk and said in a loud voice, 'Any messages for Donald Lam from Denver? I have my key.'

The clerk looked in the box back of the counter, shook his head.

I waved the key at him by way of salute and walked over to the elevator.

She didn't dare try to follow me into the elevator. That would have been pressing luck too far.

I got off at the fourth floor, hurried to the stairs, ran down to the third floor, and stood there watching the elevator indicators.

The next cage came shooting up, and the needle came to a quivering stop at the fourth floor.

I pressed the button on the down elevator, boarded it on the third floor, went down to the lobby, tossed my key onto the desk.

This would give my shadow a chance to report to her boss that she'd located my address in the downtown hotel where I was staying.

She was satisfied with herself; I was satisfied with myself; and I had Daphne Creston's three hundred dollars.

I felt I'd need a few clean clothes, so I went to my regular apartment to pack up a bag.

I knew I'd ranked the job as soon as I reached the entrance to the building.

I don't know where Sergeant Sellers had been waiting, but it was probably in a parked car. He made good time getting out and up the short flight of steps, because he was looking over my shoulder before I'd finished sorting the mail that was in my mailbox.

'Hello, Pint Size,' he said.

I didn't look up. 'Hello Frank. I smelled soggy tobacco and figured you must be around somewhere. What's new?'

'You are.'

'Whatta you mean?'

'You're news.'

'News to me.'

'It won't be. Let's go up.'

'Up where?'

'Your apartment.'

'What for?'

'I want to look around.'

'Got a warrant?' I asked.

'You're damn tooting!' Sellers said.

We went up to the apartment. I took a key from my pocket.

Sellers pushed in behind me. I could smell the half-smoked cold cigar he was chewing.

'If you don't mind, I'll take a look at the warrant,' I said.

'Suits me,' Sellers said, and handed me a copy of a search warrant, showing that he was looking for evidence of an undisclosed nature taken from 1771 Hemmet Avenue, where one Dale Dirking Finchley had been murdered.

'This warrant is no good,' I said. 'It has to describe the person or place to be searched and the thing or things to be found.'

Sellers shifted his cold cigar and grinned, 'Want to resist an officer on the strength of your objection?' he asked.

'No. I'll raise the point in court.'

'Do that. That's your privilege.'

'Just what are you looking for, Sellers?' I asked.

'A girl,' he said.

'I'm a respectable bachelor,' I told him.

'Nuts!' he said.

He started looking around the apartment, looking in the wastebasket, looking in the closet, looking under the bed. He prowled in the back part of the closet, looked carefully at the shoes, looked at the ash trays to see if he could find any cigarette stubs with lipstick on them.

'Where have you got her, Pint Size?' he asked.

'Got who?'

'The girl.'

'And the theory is that I have a girl who knows something?'

'You're concealing the girl, and you know what that's going to do.'

'What?'

'I'll tell you that,' he said, 'when your license hearing

comes up. I hate to keep picking on you Donald, because at times you *have* co-operated, and Bertha is a good egg.

'Bertha made her mistake when she went into partnership with you. Bertha was running a respectable . . .'

'Collection agency,' I interrupted.

'Well, it was on the up-and-up anyway, and Bertha didn't need to lose sleep nights wondering about her license.'

'She doesn't need to lose any sleep now,' I told him.

'Perhaps not as long as I'm her friend and *she* plays square with me,' he said.

Sellers went into the bathroom, looked at the toothbrushes, examined the bath towels, looked in the hamper for soiled clothes.

'You look for things in funny places,' I told him.

'Sometimes I find things in funny places,' he said.

'What else besides a girl?' I asked.

'Money.'

'How much money?'

'According to the tip I have, a firm of contractors was going to make bids on the construction of roads, grading, development of storm drainage and eventually all of the improvements in a big subdivision. There was to be a whole series of bids. Finchley was attorney for the subdividers.

'Bids were supposed to be accompanied by a cash deposit as evidence of good faith and performance.

'Since these deposits were returned to the unsuccessful bidders, they were usually in the form of certified checks or cashier's checks, but I'm told a group of contractors got in on the bidding at the last minute and, in order to make their bid legal, they had to send over forty thousand in cash. They phoned Finchley and got an O.K. Then they sent the money over. It could have been in the house when Finchley got in the way of a bullet.'

'Who told you all this?' I asked.

'A little bird.'

'Who are the contractors.'

Sellers looked at me and rolled the cigar stub around with his lips.

'Why do you ask?'

'Because I'd like to find out.'

Sellers said, 'Frankly, Donald, I don't know.' And then he added, 'And somehow I have the sneaking idea that perhaps *you* do. And, if you do and you've been holding out, I'll break you if it's the last damn thing I do.'

Sellers looked me over thoughtfully. 'O.K., Donald,' he said. 'I'm going to give you a chance to come clean.'

'Thank you.'

'You should thank me. A lot of cops would just lower the boom. Now, I'll tell you this much: we're looking for a woman in connection with Dale Finchley. There's evidence that a woman was in the house at the time the murder was committed. The assumption is that the woman fired the fatal shot. There's also evidence that a woman ran out of the house shortly after the fatal shot and disappeared down the street.

'We don't know where she went to, but we do know that you were cruising in the neighborhood. We know that you're a Don Quixote as far as women are concerned, and we have reason to believe that you may have taken this woman down to the Finchley home and were waiting outside for her to join you.'

'What evidence?' I asked.

'Lots of evidence,' he said. 'We don't give a suspect *all* of our evidence, you know.'

'Am I suspect?'

'Yes.'

'Thanks.'

'Not at all. . . . I'll tell you this much more: there's evidence that you got acquainted with a woman named Daphne Creston; that you called at the Travertine Hotel; that Daphne Creston was with you; that you picked up her baggage and drove away; that you were in a hurry and were acting suspiciously.

'What have you to say to that?'

'Nothing.'

'Do you deny it?'

'No.'

'Do you admit it?'

'Not altogether,' I said.

'Who is Daphne Creston?'

'I said I'm doing a job for a woman. I'm not mentioning her name.'

'Bertha doesn't know anything about it,' Sellers said. 'It wasn't a woman who came to the office. It was nothing you're doing in the regular routine of partnership affairs.'

'I've been pretty busy lately,' I said. 'I haven't had a chance to report to Bertha on all the details.'

'What kind of a job are you doing for this Daphne Creston?'

I hesitated as though on the point of telling him, then shook my head. 'It's confidential.'

'All right, Pint Size,' Sellers said; 'I've put you on notice.'

Sellers walked over to the telephone, dialed a number and said, 'Sergeant Frank Sellers talking. O.K., here's an order – 16-72-91-4, urgent! Got that? O.K., goodbye.'

Sellers twisted the cigar in his mouth, sat down in the most comfortable chair in the place as though he intended to stay for a week, said, 'Now, Donald, I don't need to to tell you that if what we've been told is true, or if any great percentage of it is true, you're in for a lot of trouble.'

'Yes,' I said, 'if I took a woman out to the Finchley residence; waited while she went in and murdered Finchley; then picked her up when she came out; hustled her back to the Travertine Hotel, where she was staying; picked up her baggage; took her out and concealed her – and if I am keeping her concealed, that could make me a guest of the state for a long, long time.'

'Exactly,' Sellers said.

'If, on the other hand,' I told him, 'I'm trying to do a job for a woman client, and it's a confidential job, I'm under no obligations to betray her confidence to the police just because Katherine Elliott is trying to make trouble for me.'

'Who did you say?' Sellers asked, pulling the soggy cigar out of his mouth and sitting upright.

'Katherine Elliott.'

'Who's she?'

'A disgruntled woman who is trying to make trouble for me.'

'What's she disgruntled about?'

I shrugged my shoulders. 'Search me. I tried to get some information for a client and received a brush-off.'

'What sort of information?'

'About a want ad covering an accident that took place on April fifteenth.'

Sellers started to put the soggy cigar back in his mouth, looked at it distastefully, got up, walked in the bathroom and flushed the cigar down the toilet.

I knew he was stalling for time.

'Can you tell me any more about that accident,' he asked, 'or about the job.'

'Bertha can tell you,' I said. 'You believe *everything* she tells you. You don't believe *anything* I tell you. Why don't you get in touch with Bertha?'

Sellers said, 'Some of that checks, Donald. I have been covering as much of your back trail as possible. Bertha told me you were working on some kind of a phony ad – that you were employed by a big association of insurance executives that were trying to chase down a perjury ring.'

'Well,' I said, 'I don't know as I would have told you that much, but if Bertha told you, it's all right. Katherine Elliott was mixed up in that ad business. I don't know just to what extent, but I do know that she took a violent dislike to me. I also know that she's been in trouble with the Better Business Bureau.'

'The hell she has!'

'That's right,' I told him. 'She'd tell you anything in order to make trouble for me because she knows I'm investigating and she's afraid that before I get through, she'll be in trouble herself.'

Sergeant Sellers walked to the window, then seated himself at the little dinette table and started drumming on the surface. 'You *could* be on the up-and-up,' he said.

'I could be.'

'Well, let's hope that you are,' Sellers said, 'because you could be in lots of trouble if you aren't, and this time you'd probably drag Bertha into it with you; and that would be bad. Bertha's tight as the bark on a tree; but she's honest and she's always co-operated with the police.'

'I've always co-operated with the police,' I said.

'You certainly have,' Sellers said, raising his finger and drawing it across his throat; 'some co-operation.'

'It's paid off,' I said, and then added, 'to you.'

'Yes,' Sellers admitted after a moment, 'it's paid off. Well, I'm going to be on my way, and I'll leave you alone for a while. But I'm warning you: keep your nose clean!'

Sellers walked to the door, turned and said, 'No hard feelings.'

'No hard feelings,' I told him.

Sellers walked out.

I knew that the order he had given over the telephone in code was an order to the dispatcher to have radio cars rush to this address and put me under surveillance as soon as I came out.

I waited a good fifteen minutes to give the police trap time to get itself set; then I took from my pocket the note which described Dennison Farley, the big winner of the Irish Sweepstakes, and gave his address as 1328 Severang Avenue.

I walked over to the bureau where I keep my .38-caliber revolver and put it on in a shoulder holster.

The thing makes a bulge in my coat no matter how I try to hang it, and for that reason I hate to carry a gun. But where I was going I thought it might be a good plan to have a bulge in my coat this time.

CHAPTER NINE

NUMBER 1328 Severang Avenue was one of the little cracker-box, high-utility type of houses which are being put in in subdivisions by contractors who have a set of four different plans and put these four houses up in a sequence, then start all over again until the unit may consist of forty houses in ten identical groups.

The one Dennison Farley was living in was one of the more moderately priced ones – two bedrooms, one bath, a combined living room and dining room, and a kitchen.

Farley was home. I could smell cooking coming from the kitchen. The guy looked hungry. He evidently hadn't eaten yet.

I could smell a cocktail on his breath.

He was a tall, broad-shouldered, God's-gift-to-women type; but his mouth was too big.

He looked down at me and said, 'And what can I do for you, Mr. Lam?'

'I'd like a few words with you in private.'

'How private?' he asked.

'Could you step outside?' I asked.

'I *could*,' he said.

'And if you could sit in my car, there wouldn't be so much possibility of our being overheard.'

'And what do you want to talk about?' he asked.

I gave him a card. I said, 'I'm a private detective.'

'Well, well, well,' he said, 'I've always wondered what you guys *really* looked like.'

He looked me over and then suddenly started to laugh.

'What's funny?' I asked.

'You are,' he said.

'Oh?'

'That's right. I see these private eyes on television and I read about them in the books, and they're great big bruisers who smash people in the puss and knock their teeth out, use a little karate and break an arm or two, dust off their hands, and then jump into bed with the Babe.'

'Well?' I asked.

'You aren't the type,' he said.

'I get by,' I said.

'I wonder how you do it,' he told me.

I turned around and put my hand in my pocket so the bulge on the coat was more noticeable.

Farley looked down at me, then sobered somewhat.

'I get you,' he said. 'Now, what do you want with me?'

'I want to talk with you.'

'You said that before.'

'About a private matter.'

'That also is a repetition.'

'It has to do with community property.'

'What about community property?'

'Daphne's property,' I said.

The guy straightened with a jerk as though I'd slapped him in the face with a wet towel. His eyes got cold and hard. His mouth clamped into a firm, straight line.

'I don't know what you're talking about,' he said.

'You want to come out in the car and listen for a while, or do you want me to take it from there?'

'Take it from there,' he said, 'and quit pestering me or I'll take that rod away from you and pound you to a pulp.'

'O.K.,' I told him, 'you're the doctor. I'm giving you a chance for the easy way out.'

I turned and started walking slowly down the cement walk toward the place where I had parked my car.

After a moment I heard heavy steps behind me; then a

big hand was on my shoulder. 'Now, look here, Lam,' he said, 'I don't want you going around with the idea you're going to stir up trouble.'

I didn't even look around. 'The trouble,' I told him, 'has already been stirred up.'

I kept right on walking, opened the door on the driver's side of the car, slid in behind the wheel.

'Now, wait a minute,' Farley said.

He ran around the car and got in on the other side. 'Perhaps you'd better tell me what this is all about,' he said.

'It's about community property,' I told him. 'You won a hundred and twenty-odd thousand dollars in the lottery. How much of that do you intend to give Daphne to make up for getting away with her bank account, leaving her holding the sack with . . .'

'Now, look here, Lam; that marriage wasn't any good. She knew it at the time. She consented to go through just a form of marriage with me so as to give her an aura of respectability with her friends.'

'Did you put that on the marriage license?' I asked.

'Don't be silly,' he said.

I said nothing.

'How much does she want?' he asked.

'I don't know,' I told him. 'I'd advise her to settle for five thousand dollars if I had the cash in hand to back up the offer.'

'Five thousand dollars!' he exclaimed. 'Are you crazy? Do you know how much of that winning was left after the government got done dipping its big hand into my pocket?'

'That's why I said five thousand,' I said. 'Otherwise I'd have said fifty.'

'Now, look, Lam, I'm married. I've got a daughter seven years old. She's a cute kid. Think what it would mean to her if . . .'

'If I spilled the beans?' I asked.

'Exactly,' he said.

'You should have thought of her when you were putting the beans on the stove,' I told him.

'Now, look, Lam, I'm a salesman. I'm away from home a good deal, and when I'm away from home I'm just like any human male animal. But I love my wife and I love my kid, and I wouldn't do anything to hurt them.'

'Well, that's fine,' I told him. 'If you haven't done anything to hurt them, you have nothing to be afraid of.'

'I didn't mean it that way. I meant that sometimes a fellow gets crummy impulses. He does things he's ashamed of afterwards, but he doesn't do them deliberately. It's all on the spur of the moment.'

'I see,' I told him.

'You may see; but do you understand?'

'Sure, I understand,' I said, 'and, furthermore, I understand that if you're going to do anything like the square thing, you'll get five thousand dollars for Daphne.'

'The way I look at it, she's not entitled to a cent. She went into this with her eyes open.'

'The way I look at it, she's entitled to a lot more,' I said. 'You bamboozled her into a bigamous marriage. She was too compassionate and forgiving to prosecute you. But when you had the good fortune to win a big stake at the lottery, she became forcibly reminded of the joint account that you took when you skipped out.'

'It was only a little over eleven hundred dollars,' he said. 'I'll give that back to her. I've intended to do that all along. I was hard up for cash at the time, and I – well, I just cleaned out the account, partially because I needed the money and partially because I didn't want her to have money to ... to ...'

'To what?' I asked.

'To hire some goddamned private detective,' he blurted.

'Exactly,' I said. 'Now she's hired a goddamned private detective and it's going to cost you five thousand bucks at the very least. And I'm not sure I can get her to settle for that.'

'I can't do it.'

'Suit yourself,' I told him. 'You can . . .'

A police car drove up and parked alongside.

Sergeant Frank Sellers, a comparatively fresh cigar in his mouth, got out of the car and came walking around.

'Well, Pint Size,' he said, 'you *have* taken us on a little chase. Let's find out what *this* is all about.'

Sellers showed his identification card to Farley. 'What's your name?' he asked.

'What's all this about?' Farley asked.

'What's your name?' Sellers said. 'And don't take all day trying to think up an alias.'

'Dennison Farley.'

'How long have you known this guy Donald Lam?'

'I just met him.'

'What does he want?'

'It's a private matter.'

'I said what does he want?'

Farley hesitated.

A good-looking woman came to the door of Farley's house, looked out and saw him sitting in my car, with the police car parked alongside. She started to say something, turned back in the house, then turned back toward the porch again and stood there watching.

'Well?' Sellers said.

Farley said, 'This guy is a private detective. He's trying to make a collection for a broad I got tangled up with some months ago in a Middle Western state.'

'What's her name?' Sellers asked.

'That doesn't need to enter into it. It . . .'

'What's her name?' Sellers snapped.

'Daphne Creston,' Farley said.

'Well, I'll be damned!' Sellers muttered.

'This thing is first cousin to blackmail,' Farley went on.

'What threats have I made?' I asked.

'That's neither here nor there.'

'Have I made any threats?'

'You've talked about trouble.'

'Did I spell out the kind of trouble?'

'Well, no.'

'Did I threaten to prosecute you if you didn't do what I wanted?'

'I thought there was an innuendo.'

'Forget it,' I told him. 'I'm making no threats. I'm representing a woman who has an equitable claim on you, and if you have a spark of decency, you'll pay off. If you haven't, I can't help you; and, furthermore, I want it understood that I'm not holding out the promise that no action will taken if you accede to her demands.'

'Say, what *is* all this about?' Sellers asked.

'It's a little family trouble, Sergeant.'

Farley pulled a checkbook from his pocket. 'All right,' he said. 'I make this check to Daphne Creston for five thousand bucks. I put on it "in full of all claims of any sort, legal, equitable, or otherwise." '

'O.K.,' I said, 'I'll give her the check. After she cashes it, if it's good, you'll have a receipt. If she sends it back to you, you'll know she isn't making a settlement at that figure.'

'Well, she damned well better make a settlement at that figure. She couldn't get a penny more no matter what she did.'

Sellers stood there while Farley made out the check and handed it to me.

I said, 'O.K., you'll be hearing from me. You got a telephone?'

'Yes, it's unlisted.'

'Put the telephone number on the check.'

He wrote the number on the check.

I said, 'O.K.' Then I turned to Sellers. 'What are you doing out here, Frank?'

'I just thought I'd better keep you from getting into any more trouble,' Sellers said.

'I didn't see you following me.'

'You're damned right you didn't,' Sellers said. 'It was an

expert job, and I didn't do it. It was done from a helicopter.'

Farley had been listening with big ears. He said to Sellers, 'Just who is this guy?'

'He told you,' Sellers said. 'His name is Donald Lam. He's a private detective, and the son of a bitch is smart.'

With that he turned away.

CHAPTER TEN

WHEN Bertha Cool once got away from the office she loved to lounge around her apartment, wearing pajamas, slippers and a silk robe, listening to classical music on a hi-fi.

It was always difficult for me to reconcile this picture of Bertha with her attitude in the office when she was encased in a girdle, sitting erect in a creaky swivel chair, her eyes as hard as the diamonds on her fingers, trying to squeeze every last cent of profit out of everything she touched.

I knew that Bertha hated to be disturbed by business affairs after she had left the office, but we were in a jam and there was no other way out.

I called her on her unlisted telephone.

When she answered I could hear the dreamy strains of Beethoven's Sixth Symphony.

'Donald talking, Bertha,' I said.

'Where the hell have you been?'

'Working.'

'What do you want?'

'I have to see you.'

'Tomorrow.'

'Now.'

'All right, come ahead if you *have* to.'

'It's that important,' I told her.

'It had better be,' she said, and hung up.

I drove around to Bertha's apartment, a place devoted to sheer physical luxury – heavy drapes; subdued, indirect lighting; soft reclining chairs; and the smell of incense.

Bertha greeted me at the door with her finger on her lips, said in a subdued voice, 'Come in and sit down and don't talk until this number is finished.'

Bertha melted her figure into a reclining chair, settled back, closed her eyes, and waited with a beatific smile on her face, soaking up the music as a tired golfer might soak up the luxury of a hot bath.

When the record was finished, Bertha pressed a button, the hi-fi clicked off, and Bertha glared at me with beady-eyed hostility.

'I hate to be interrupted at night with matters of business, Donald.'

'I know.'

'What do you want?'

'I want to dissolve the partnership.'

'What?' she asked, the words rasping out of her throat as she started to struggle to an upright posture.

'I want to dissolve the partnership.'

'What have I done now? God knows I've put up with your shenanigans . . . you should . . .'

'It isn't what you've done,' I told her; 'it's what I've done.'

'What have you done?'

'I've got in a jam where I'm going to lose my license, and there's no need for both of us losing it.'

'You sound as if you've been talking with Frank Sellers.'

'He's been talking with me.'

'I see,' Bertha said; and then added after a moment, 'There *is* a difference.'

I said, 'It's this damned automobile-ad case. There's something in there that's mighty fishy.

'I went to a lot of trouble and quite a bit of expense building up an identity for myself and then called on this number in the Monadnock Building. A girl by the name of Katherine Elliott is running one of these fly-by-night offices where you can rent an office for an hour or probably for fifteen minutes.

'A man by the name of Harper interviewed me. I did a good job of it, letting him know that I'd be available for a perjured affidavit if he'd kick through with three hundred bucks.

'I thought I had the sale made, but there was another person who had answered the ad – a girl named Daphne Creston. And as soon as I saw her I knew that I might have trouble because she was just exactly what they were looking for – a green kid, naïve, and down on her luck.

'So I decided to have a second string to my bow. I made it a point to get acquainted with Daphne.

'Sure enough, they passed me up in favor of Daphne and gave me the old brush-off.

'So I started working through Daphne and found out that Rodney Harper was actually a man named Walter Lucas – of the very prominent contracting firm of Lathrop, Lucas and Manly.

'In the meantime, our client, Barney Adams, has some kind of an in with Katherine Elliott. I imagine that he's bribed her to tell him all she knows.

'He found out through her that I had been given the brush-off, and that made him mad. After all, he'd put up quite a little dough to get a line on the situation through me, and he didn't want to kiss that money goodbye.'

'It wasn't our fault,' Bertha said, 'if another sucker showed up. What the hell did the guy expect – infallibility?'

'That's *exactly* what he expected,' I told her. 'Infallibility.'

'Well, you're sitting pretty if you've got a line on this Daphne Creston – and, knowing you as I do, I have a hunch that if this babe is naïve and impressionable she's looking up at your infinite wisdom with starry-eyed worship.'

'I've kept in touch with her,' I admitted.

'Where is she now?' Bertha asked.

'In an apartment I rented as a hide-out.'

'Under what name?'

'My own, fortunately.'

'Why fortunately?'

'Because,' I said, 'this whole thing is mixed up in a murder case in some way, and the reason they wanted a patsy was to deal with Dale Finchley.

'They took Daphne Creston out to Finchley's house. They told her to go in and pick up a brief case, Daphne went in. Finchley was getting murdered at just about the time Daphne went in. The man she knew as Rodney Harper got wise, high-tailed it out of there, and left her to face the music. But she was smart enough to get out of the house, avoid the police, and get back to me. But the police know some woman was in the house, and this Katherine Elliott is shooting off her big mouth, trying to get even with me because I went to the Better Business Bureau to check on her operations. So, all in all, it's a sweet mess.'

Bertha closed her eyes for a little while, thinking; then she said, 'What the hell, Donald! A big contracting firm wouldn't lay themselves wide open, spend three hundred bucks, and go to all this rigmarole simply in order to get a patsy.'

'They would, and they did,' I said. 'That means it had to be something big. They thought that they might be walking into a trap. So they'd send somebody into that trap who was willing to commit downright perjury for three hundred bucks. There was, of course, big money at stake in this contracting deal.'

'How much money?'

I said, 'The brief case Daphne picked up contained forty thousand bucks.'

'Fry me for an oyster!' Bertha said.

'Exactly,' I said, 'and it *may* have been the wrong brief case at that.'

Bertha was silent for a while. Then she asked, 'What does Sergeant Sellers know about this babe?'

'Not too much,' I said. 'He knows that she's my client. He knows that I was somewhere near the Finchley house at the time Finchley was getting murdered.'

'What the hell were you doing down there then?'

'Following the car that had Daphne Creston in it.'

'You got yourself in a sweet mess,' Bertha said.

'That's why I'm here.'

'I'm surprised Sellers didn't take you down to headquarters and shake you down.'

'He would have, if it hadn't been for one thing.'

'What's that?'

'Daphne Creston's husband – a husband by a bigamous marriage, incidentally – who won the Irish Sweepstakes and got his picture in the paper.

'I knew that Frank Sellers would be trailing me to find out where Daphne Creston fitted into the picture. I went out and put the bite on Daphne's husband just for the sake of building up an alibi. I thought that he might try beating up on me, but I came just as close to blackmail as I dared; and then Sergeant Sellers showed up and the husband thought I had police backing, so he caved in and that's that.'

'How much did you nick him for?' Bertha asked.

'Five grand.'

'You little bastard!' Bertha said admiringly.

'But,' I said, 'this thing is all mixed up. This Katherine Elliott is running a fly-by-night office, and the Better Business Bureau doesn't like her, and Barney Adams has been trying to bribe her, probably with some success, so he could find out what the ad is is all about and . . .'

'What's Adams' hookup?' she asked.

'I don't know,' I told her, 'and I wish I did. This business of his representing a combination of insurance companies is just so much baloney.'

Bertha was silent again, and then said, 'This Daphne Creston – is she good-looking?'

'Tops.'

'I should have known,' Bertha commented. 'Why do I always ask such goddamned foolish questions?'

'I'd have co-operated in any event,' I said. 'She had to be the second string to my bow.'

'She wasn't a string to your bow,' Bertha said. 'She was a

beau on your string! God Almighty, I'm getting crude. That's a hell of a way to make a pun.'

'She's a good kid, Bertha,' I said.

'What else have you done for her?'

'I collected three hundred bucks for her.'

'Cash?'

'Cash.'

'What about the five grand?'

'A check.'

'Payable to us or to Daphne?'

'To Daphne. In full of account.'

'Daphne know anything about this?'

'No, and I don't dare to tell her.'

'Why not?'

'I think they're shadowing me. I'm hotter than a stove lid.'

'What do you want me to do?'

'Get yourself in the clear, Bertha. We'll dissolve the partnership as of now. We'll make a written declaration and date it, and we'll call in a witness and you can show it to Sergeant Sellers . . .'

'Don't be silly,' Bertha said. 'I'm a cantankerous old bitch, but I don't leave a partner on a sinking ship. The hell with that stuff.'

'This,' I said, 'could be serious. Usually I can see a way out, but this time I can't see a way out. And this Katherine Elliott is trying to do everything she can to get me in trouble on the theory that if I'm in enough trouble I can't make trouble for her.'

Bertha's jaw pushed forward a little. 'All right,' she said, 'we'll take care of this Katherine Elliott.'

'It isn't going to be that simple,' I said.

'Everything is simple,' Bertha said, 'when one woman deals face to face with another woman. It's when women are dealing with men that the situation becomes complicated.

'Women are creatures of intrigue. They love to set obscure

causes in motion to bring about results that will take place behind the scenes. Women love to make-believe. They put on mascara, false eyelashes, bird's-nests in their hair falsies on front, and bustles on behind.

'They live their lives the same way. They use subtleties and accomplish what they want by indirection. When some woman who is a believer in direct methods enters the picture and strips off the falsies from these sirens they go all to pieces.

'I'll go to this Katherine What's-her-name and tell the bitch where she gets off, and don't think I won't. You happen to know her home address?'

'Yes. She's in the Steelbuilt Apartments. I got her address from my friend Evelyn Calhoun.'

'Another woman,' Bertha said.

'Another woman.'

'Friend of yours?'

'Yes.'

'Who is she?'

'Secretary for the Better Business Bureau. She'll co-operate with us on anything reasonable, but we'll have to deal her in because she has been laying for the type of operation Katherine Elliott carries on. They had a run-in once before, and she told Katherine to keep her nose clean.'

Bertha said, almost musingly, 'I'd better go see Katherine Elliott and give her a going over.'

'I don't think so, Bertha,' I said. 'Not yet, anyway. We've got to know more about what the picture is before we start rubbing too many people the wrong way.

'That's one thing about this whole deal that bothers me: it's big whatever it is and the people we're working with so far are pawns.'

Bertha thought for a moment, then said, 'This Daphne Creston what about her?'

I said, 'The poor kid has about thirty-five cents to her name.'

'And a brief case with forty thousand bucks?' Bertha asked.

'In cash,' I said.

'Who knows she has that?'

'Walter Lucas, for one, may know that she has it with her.'

'And what's this Daphne Creston doing for living expenses?'

'I had my dummy apartment provisioned up. She's living there. At least I hope she is. I told her not to go out under any circumstances.'

'And Sergeant Sellers knows you've collected five grand for her?'

I nodded.

'He'll be watching to see what happens to that five grand,' she said.

I nodded.

'So what do you do?' Bertha asked.

'So,' I said, 'I get hold of Elsie Brand. I write Daphne Creston a very impersonal letter: "My dear Miss Creston: It will interest you to know that we have been in touch with your former husband, so-called, and secured from him settlement in an amount of five thousand dollars.

' "The check is payable to you in full of account. We are enclosing it herewith and suggest that, if the amount is satisfactory to you and bearing in mind that it represents a complete settlement of all financial affairs between yourself and your former husband, you cash the check and then get in touch with us for an adjustment of our fees in the matter." '

'And how do you send that?' Bertha asked.

'Through the United States mails, special delivery, leaving a carbon copy in our files. And if Sergeant Sellers comes down with a search warrant to search our files for anything, he finds this letter and . . .'

'And gets the address,' Bertha said.

'And gets the address,' I told her.

'Do you want him to have that?'

'No, I can't afford to let him have that until . . .'

'Until what?'

'Until the case is solved.'

'But you just said he's going to get it.'

'That's right. He'll get it, but it will be probably twenty-four hours before he can get it.'

'And you mean that in that time you've got to have the case solved?'

'In that time I want to have the case solved.'

'What case?'

'I'm very much afraid,' I said, 'it's the murder of Dale Finchley. At least that's mixed up in it enough so that I can't be sure of anything until I know what happened there.'

Bertha shook her head. 'You can't do it. The police are working on that case tooth and nail. You stick your neck in there and you'll be sucked into a vortex of activity that will bust you wide open.'

'What else can I do?' I asked.

'Sit tight,' Bertha said.

I said, 'Frank Sellers is going to be at the office. He's going to want to look for our files in the case of Daphne Creston. He'll ask us to produce the files as evidence of good faith. We'll tell him we can't do it because it's a confidential matter with a client. And he'll then demand that we produce them on the ground that they may be evidence in a murder case.'

'All right,' Bertha said; 'use that ingenuity of yours. How are we going to stop him?'

'We can't stop him.'

'All right, then; how are we going to confuse him?'

'That isn't what I came up here for, Bertha. I want to get you in the clear.'

'To hell with that stuff. We're in this together. Now, use that noggin of yours to get this thing straightened out, and then get the hell out of there and let me soak up some more music.'

'Well,' I said, 'we could write Daphne at General Delivery and send the letter there and then get Elsie to pick up the letter at General Delivery under the name of Daphne

Creston and take the letter to Daphne at the apartment. They wouldn't be shadowing Elsie Brand early in the morning.'

'You know the number of Elsie's phone and her apartment?' Bertha asked.

I nodded.

'You would,' Bertha said; and then added, 'Get her on the phone. I'll talk to her.'

'She may have a date,' I said.

'Then we'll call her when she gets in. She'll be at the apartment sometime tonight.'

'Presumably,' I said.

'She isn't the type of girl who stays out all night,' Bertha said. 'Not unless you're involved. My heavens, the way that girl looks at you! She follows you with her eyes around the office. . . . It looks like hell. Why don't you get rid of her and get some homely, hatchet-faced. . . . No, you wouldn't be happy – and if you got some other girl, it would be the same way. I don't know what the hell it is you do to women, but I guess it's because you don't fall all over yourself making passes at them. You just go about your business, and it's a challenge to them.'

Bertha pointed an imperious finger. 'Hand me that telephone, Donald.'

I handed her the phone and gave her Elsie Brand's number.

Bertha called and, after a few moments, had Elsie on the line.

'Take your pencil, Elsie,' she said, 'I want to dictate a letter to you. I want you take it in shorthand. You ready?'

Bertha dictated the letter to Daphne Creston.

'Now, I want you to address that to Daphne Creston – General Delivery. I want you to go to the office right now and type it, and before you get it finished Donald will be in there with five thousand bucks to put in the letter. Then he'll tell you what else to do first thing tomorrow morning before you come to work. Got it?

'Yes, he's all right. . . . Yes, he's right here. . . . Yes, of course he's all right. . . . Oh, my God, hang onto the phone.'

Bertha turned to me disgustedly. 'She wants to hear you say that everything's all right,' she said.

I picked up the telephone, said, 'Hello, Elsie. I'm all right.'

'Donald, I've been worried.'

'Why?'

'I don't know. Call it a woman's intuition, if you want, but – you *are* in some kind of trouble, aren't you, Donald?'

'Forget it,' I told her. 'I'm always in trouble. Go up to the office and I'll meet you up there. We'll get that letter out, and I'll give you a check to put in it – also three nice new crisp one-hundred-dollar bills.'

'Isn't that risky sending money that way through the mail?'

'Yes.'

'Then why do it, Donald? I could take it.'

'That would be even more risky. I'll be seeing you at the office. Don't worry, Elsie. Everything is all right.'

I hung up the telephone. Bertha shook her head. 'That girl has put you up on a pedestal, and I don't suppose there's anything you can do about it except get the relationship on a more mundane, normal basis, and that would present even more problems.'

'And so?' I asked.

'And so,' Bertha said, 'you'll have to put up with it. It would drive me nuts, having someone looking starry-eyed at me that way. But don't try to make an operative out of her, Donald, because she isn't the type.'

'I know.'

Bertha grunted. 'Why don't you make passes at them and get your face slapped once in a while? It's a more normal relationship.'

'Suppose they don't slap?'

Bertha thought that over and said, 'It probably would undermine office efficiency.' And then, after a moment, she added, 'But it's undermined anyway. Get the hell out of here and let me listen to some music.'

'Sellers is on the warpath,' I told her.

'How long have we got?'

'Perhaps twenty-four hours as an extreme limit. You know Sellers. He may come down like a ton of bricks at any time. I've stalled him off for a while – probably twelve to twenty-four hours.'

Bertha sighed. 'That'll give me time to listen to music,' she said, 'and time for you to think up one of those damned ingenious schemes that always gets us out of trouble. One of these days you're going to get caught.'

'That's what I'm trying to tell you. This may be the day.'

'All right,' Bertha said; 'I was running a collection agency until you came along, and you've scared the pants off me ever since, but I could retire if I had to. I couldn't keep up this apartment. I'd have to have a hole in the wall somewhere.'

'If you would only dissolve the partnership . . .'

'To hell with that noise,' Bertha said. 'Get out of here and go to work.'

I let myself out of the apartment. As I closed the door I heard the strains of a Strauss waltz calming Bertha's ruffled nerves.

CHAPTER ELEVEN

ELSIE BRAND had the letter all typed by the time I got to the office.

'Donald,' she said, 'who is Daphne Creston? We don't have any record of her here at the office.'

'I know,' I said. 'She contacted me on the outside. Bertha knows about her.'

'Oh.'

'I collected five grand for her. Also three hundred smackers in the form of cash. Put them in this letter and send it care of General Delivery.

'Now then, tomorrow you go to the General Delivery window at the Post Office and leave a change of address. Say that you're Daphne Creston.'

'What's the address?'

I gave her a card on which I had printed in pen and ink the number of the apartment I was renting as a hide-out.

'This Miss Creston has an apartment here?'

I nodded.

'Under her own name?'

'Well,' I said, 'she may be using another name. She's trying to keep under cover – probably is – but this letter will get to her. Tell you what we'll do: we'll cut out the General Delivery stuff on the envelope and send it to her at this address Special Delivery. Make it care of Donald Lam – and at that address. But leave the address on our carbon copy as General Delivery. We'll just take it down and drop it in the post office.'

'Not in the mail chute?'

'No, we'll get more direct action if we take it to the post office.'

'We could use the mail chute right here in the building. There's a collection at ten o'clock tonight.'

'You're sure of that?'

'Of course. I make it a rule to keep posted on the times of mail pickup.'

'Well, that's swell, Elsie,' I told her. 'We won't have to attract attention by going to a post office. If we do that and we should be followed, they'll know we're mailing an important letter. And you can't tell just what Sergeant Sellers may do.'

'Sergeant Sellers. Is he in this?'

'He's in everything that involves me,' I said. 'He's always inclined to snoop around on my back trail whenever he has something bothering him.'

'And something is bothering him now?'

I nodded.

'Donald, is it the Finchley murder?'

'Could be,' I said. 'Heaven knows what it is that bothers him, but whenever something turns up Frank Sellers wants to know what I'm doing first rattle out of the box.'

'Well, we'll just fool him. We'll drop it in the mail chute right now,' she said, 'and send it Special Delivery and then you can take me out for a bite to eat; and if you're being shadowed it will look as though we simply made a rendezvous here at the office.'

'Fair enough,' I told her.

'Unless you think I'm forward – inviting myself out to dinner with you.'

'You have a standing invitation,' I said. 'All you need to do is to let me know when you can accept.'

'Donald, you're *so* nice.'

We sealed the envelope, put a Special Delivery stamp on it, made certain there was no one on that floor of the office building at that hour of the evening, dropped the envelope in the mail chute, and went to dinner.

After dinner, I took Elsie home.

'Coming in, Donald?'

I looked at my watch, said, 'I'd better not. I've got quite a day tomorrow.'

'Promise me you won't get into any trouble.'

'I'll try not to.'

She put up her face to be kissed good night; and I climbed in my car and drove out to Hemmet Avenue to look around.

Finchley had lived at 1771 Hemmet. There was only a distance of some half-dozen blocks to prowl.

Number 1369 answered the description of the house Daphne had given me. It was a large-two-story house, dating back to an older time when domestic help was easy to come by and people went in for elbow room rather than crowded efficiency.

There was a 'FOR SALE' sign on the lawn and the place was dark.

I climbed up to the porch and tried the door. It was locked.

I went to a front window, waited until I felt the coast was clear, then used a pocket electric flashlight to send a thin but powerful beam through the glass.

I could see that the place was unfurnished. I went back to my car, copied the telephone number from the sign.

Fortunately, the sign said, 'FOR SALE BY OWNER.'

I gave the number a buzz.

A man's voice answered.

'You'll forgive me for calling at this hour of the night,' I said, 'but you have a place for sale at 1369 Hemmet. Can you tell me what you want for it?'

'Who is this talking?'

'A prospective customer.'

'Do you care to leave a name?'

'No.'

'I'm not certain I care to price the place on that basis.'

'Don't be silly,' I said; 'you have a "for sale" sign; you want to sell the place. I'm in the market for a place something like this, provided it isn't too high.'

'How high are you prepared to go?' he asked.

'I want to get a good value. What is that – a four-bedroom house?'

'Four bedrooms, three and a half baths.'

'How much?'

'I have a cash price of forty-one thousand dollars. It's a big lot.'

'Is the place furnished?'

'Definitely not.'

'I'm sorry I called you at this hour of the night,' I said, 'but I'm interested. Would it be possible to get the keys to the place?'

'Not tonight. How does it happen that you're calling at this hour?'

'I'm a working man and I have only a certain amount of time after work to look around. This place looks pretty good to me. I'm trying to deal directly with owners because I feel I can save a real-estate commission that way.'

'You can, indeed, on this place,' the man said. 'But I want the whole thing in cash. That's why I'm handling it myself. The real-estate people tell me it's impossible in the present market to sell a house like that for all cash.'

'I can pay cash if I find the place I want,' I said. 'In fact, I'd rather pay cash – only I've got to have the price right if I'm putting it all on the line.'

'This price is right. The house would sell for forty-eight thousand dollars on today's market with a down payment and a trust deed.'

I said, 'I'm looking at another house tomorrow night. I . . . is there any way I can see it tonight?'

'Tell you what I'll do,' the man said. 'My name's Kelton. Olney Kelton. I'll come and meet you there if you're seriously interested.'

'I'm seriously interested.'

'You're at the house now?'

'I'm at a telephone in a nearby service station.'

'I'll be right down and meet you at the house.'

'Fair enough,' I told him.

I drove back to the house, parked in the driveway and had been there about three minutes when Kelton showed up.

He was a stoop-shouldered individual with keen eyes, a heavily-lined face, and had the look of a dyspeptic.

'My name's Lam,' I told him. 'Since you're good enough to give me your name and come down here with the keys, there's no reason why we shouldn't get acquainted.'

He fitted a key to the front door. 'You'll like this house,' he said.

'It isn't furnished?'

'No,' he said, and then, after a moment, added, 'heavens no, not at that price.'

'What about the utilities?' I asked.

'They're all hooked up,' he said. 'I show the house at night sometimes. I have your trouble. I'm working during the daytime; ordinarily I don't show it this late.'

He unlocked the door, reached in and switched on the light.

We entered the echoing corridor, walked into a spacious living room, through that into a dining room, and then I stopped abruptly in the doorway.

'What's all this?' I asked.

He frowned. 'Hang it,' he said. 'That man was supposed to have that stuff all out of here today.'

'What in the world is it?' I asked.

'The man wanted a temporary office where he could make some copies. He rented this on a forty-eight-hour basis with the understanding that he could put his copying machinery in here and would have it moved out at the end of forty-eight hours.'

'Well, I'll be darned,' I said. 'This is modern, up-to-the-minutes copying stuff, and there's a whole battery of machines here. You could feed papers in here and get electronic copies – now, what in the world would a man want to do anything like that for?'

'I don't know,' he said. 'The guy's name is Harper, and he's got an office here in town. He said he had some papers he was going to want to copy and made me a very satisfactory offer.'

'Well, I'll be darned,' I said; 'that certainly is strange, isn't it?'

'Oh, I don't know,' Kelton said. 'There's no office space for rent around here, and this guy wanted a room which wasn't all cluttered up with household furniture. Now, here's the kitchen out this way, and there are two bedrooms on the lower floor. I told you there are four bedrooms in the house. Actually, there are five. There's a maid's room downstairs in the basement, a very nice comfortable little room with a toilet and shower.'

'The other bedrooms are upstairs?' I asked.

'Two bedrooms and a big front room which can be made into a bedroom. The people who lived here had the husband's father living with them, and he had one of the upstairs bedrooms and this sitting room. The people lived downstairs. The father passed on, and it's a big house and . . . You have a family, Mr. Lam?'

'I'm thinking of acquiring a family,' I said.

He looked at me, and I said, 'I'm marrying a divorced woman who has five children.'

'Oh – oh!' he said.

I went on hurriedly. 'I've known her for a long time, and when her marriage split up, I – well, I think we could make a go of it.'

'This house is *exactly* what you should have,' he said.

I said, 'I want to do a little remodeling.'

'That wouldn't be difficult. That upstairs room could be made into a good sitting room for the children.'

'How old is the place?'

'It was built in thirty-two at a time when you could get really good materials and good workmanship cheap. The

Depression was on and people were really looking for work and the lumberyards were looking for business. The man who owned the lot had money, and he decided it was a good time to put up a house.'

I nodded.

We went up the stairs to the upper floor, then up a flight of stairs to an attic.

I said, 'I'd like to have my intended look at this place. I think it may suit.'

'Well, that can be arranged all right.'

'She's working,' I said. 'Look here, how about letting me have the key and . . .'

He shook his head. 'I'm not tying the place up for as much as ten minutes,' he said, 'not without a down payment.'

'All right,' I told him. 'I'll give you a down payment of a hundred dollars for a twenty-four-hour option on the place at thirty-eight thousand five hundred dollars cash. You let me have a key, and the understanding will be that if I don't take the place, you're a hundred dollars ahead. And if I do, the hundred dollars goes on the purchase price.'

He recoiled. 'Not for no thirty-eight thousand five hundred,' he said. 'Why, this place is worth . . .'

'I know,' I told him, 'but I have to figure what it's worth to me, not what it's worth on the market. I'm looking for a home.'

'You've got a home right here,' he said.

'Could be,' I told him.

'Forty-one thousand is the price, cash. I'm not much of a horse trader.'

'I'm a very poor horse trader myself,' I said. 'I don't know what the place is worth on the market. I don't know what it's worth to you. It's worth thirty-eight five to me, *if* the little woman approves of it and the children like it.'

'You haven't looked at the yard,' he said.

'That's what you think,' I told him. 'I sized the place up before you got here.'

He hesitated a moment, then said, 'I'll take your deal on a basis of thirty-nine five.'

I shook my head and started for the door.

'Thirty-nine,' he said.

'I'm sorry, Mr. Kelton, but thirty-eight five is my limit.'

'I hadn't intended to sell the place that cheap. Shucks, I could have listed it with a real-estate firm and come out as well or even better . . .'

'This is cash,' I said, 'all cash.'

'When?' he asked.

'Tomorrow night at midnight you'll either have a hundred dollars to the good or I'll have a check payable to the escrow company for thirty-eight four and you can apply the hundred dollars against the purchase price.'

'Where's the hundred?' he asked.

I took out my wallet and pulled out a hundred-dollar bill.

Kelton went back down to the dining room, where the copying equipment was set up; leaned on a stand which held a copy machine; and made out a receipt.

I studied the receipt and held out my hand for the key.

Kelton dropped the key in my hand.

'Midnight tomorrow,' he said.

'Midnight tomorrow,' I told him.

'Of course, that's the technical time limit,' he said, 'but you'll know before that, and I'd like to know before that. I don't want to be disturbed at midnight by a telephone.'

'You won't be,' I told him. 'I'm just making that at midnight so I can have a reasonable length of time. Women sometimes take a little time to make up their minds.'

'I know. I know,' he said, and then, after a moment, muttered grumblingly, 'I'll say they do.'

I pocketed the key and the receipt.

'I really should have some references,' he said at length.

I gave him the name of my banker, then asked, 'What about all this junk that's in here? Are they going to move that out?'

'It's supposed to be out already.'

'I want it understood that I have no responsibility for any of that stuff.'

'Of course you don't. They put it in and they were supposed to have it out before this.'

'Harper you said the man's name was?'

'Yes.'

'Got any references on *him*?' I asked.

'Some office in the Monadnock Building. I've got the number written down at home ... said the guy was absolutely all right, a hundred per cent ... There must be several thousand dollars' worth of copying equipment here.'

'At least,' I said. 'This Harper has a key?' I asked.

'Oh, yes. He's supposed to have that material all out of the place. He has to have a key so he can move it.'

'You said you had a reference?'

'Yes, of course, an office in the Monadnock Building.'

I said, 'He must be quite a big businessman.'

'I gather he has rather an extensive office,' Kelton said.

'He must have,' I said, 'if he could take all of this equipment out of his office without imparing the efficiency of operations. Don't you think we should take an inventory so we could protect ourselves?'

Kelton shook his head. 'I'm protected,' he said. 'I drew up the receipts so I was protected. And, as far as you're concerned, this material has nothing to do with you.'

'Suppose this man Harper claims I stole some of the machines?'

'He'd have to prove it.'

'He could say they were missing.'

'Missing means nothing. He'd have to prove you took them.'

I said, 'I think I'll make an inventory just the same.'

'Well,' Kelton said, 'I'm not going to wait around while you do it. You can do it if you want to, but I'm in the clear and it's late and I don't propose to hang around here making a senseless inventory. If Harper doesn't get the stuff out of here tomorrow morning, I'm going to charge him a hundred dollars a day rental and put a rental lien on the machinery.'

'All right,' I said; 'I'll come back and take an inventory.'

'It won't do you any good without a witness,' Kelton pointed out. 'Harper can say that you took one or two machines and *then* made the inventory.'

'Yes, I suppose so, but – there's no chance of getting you to help me on this thing? It will protect us both.'

'Oh, all right,' he said grudgingly. 'Let's make a record of the number of machines that are here. We can at least make a count of numbers without going to the trouble of getting brand names, model numbers, and all of that stuff. Now, let's see, there are two machines on this side of the room, two machines on that side, one in the centre. There are an even five machines here, and they're all for copying. At least that's what they seem to be made for.'

'That's right,' I said. 'We have five machines if you only figure numbers and not detailed descriptions.'

'All right, I'll remember that. That's all of an inventory you need, Lam. That stuff will be out of here in the morning.'

'I'd like to have it out of here before my bride-to-be takes a look,' I said. 'She might get an erroneous idea of the room and the adaptability of the house.'

'O.K. O.K., have it your own way. We've got five machines here, all on tables. Now let's go home.'

'How did he move this stuff in – with a van?' I asked.

'He must have. You don't load equipment like this in the back of an automobile.'

Kelton led the way and, as we went out, closed the front door, which had a spring lock. He went down to the curb, got in his car and drove away.

I went back into the house, switched on the lights, and went over the place carefully.

I couldn't find a thing except those confounded machines

– each one resting on a table, each table having a drawer supplied with a large quantity of copying paper. I took serial numbers and model numbers of all five of the machines.

I had just finished when I heard the distant scream of a siren. It was getting louder.

I made a run for it, turning out lights as I went.

I had just reached the front door when a car went screaming by. It was going too fast for me to get any idea of anything other than a dark-colored sedan going like hell.

Behind it, at a distance of forty or fifty yards, came a police car – the red light on, the siren wailing.

The lead car suddenly made a turn into the side street. I thought for a second it was going to tip over. The tires shrieked into a skid; the car tilted far over on the springs, all but grazed the opposite curb, then straightened and tore down the street and into another turn. I couldn't see the other turn, but I could hear the scream of the tires.

The police car was expertly driven. It took the turn, its own tires skidding and screaming. Then the police car straightened and roared into speed.

At the next corner, I listened to see if the police car made the turn.

Instead of the sound of rubber tires sliding over the pavement, I heard the sound of three shots.

My car was parked at the curb. I moved it just far enough to find a parking place about a half a block down the street and then sat there in the darkened car.

After a while more police cars came. They started patrolling the neighborhood.

Still more police cars were thrown into the area. Suddenly, a spotlight blinded my eyes. A police car drew alongside.

'What are you doing here?' an officer asked.

'Waiting.'

'What for?'

'What for! By God, how can you ask that? I get half a block at a time and then some police car forces me into the curb with a siren. I'm waiting until you finish with whatever you're doing here so I can go home.'

'I'll just check your driver's license,' the officer said.

I wearily showed him my driver's license.

The officer suddenly jerked to attention. 'Lam!' he said. 'Donald Lam! Didn't you figure in this case in some way?'

'What case are you talking about?'

'You a friend of Sergeant Sellers?'

'I know him.'

'You . . . just a minute. You wait there.'

The officer went back to his car and used his communications system. He was back after four or five minutes, and his manner had undergone quite a change.

'What are you doing down in this neighborhood?' he asked.

'Working on a case.'

'You have a case in this neighborhood?'

'Yes.'

'What is it?'

'Sergeant Sellers knows about it. I've been making a collection.'

'Sellers said you've already made the collection.'

'I've done part of the job. There's other stuff I have to do.'

The officer, said, 'I'm sorry, Lam, but I've got to take a look.'

'At what?'

'You. Get out and stand up facing the car; put your hands on the back of the car.'

'You mean you're going to search me?'

'I mean I'm going to search you.'

'You have no right to.'

'I have no alternative other than to make a search. You're figuring in this case.'

'What case?'

'You know. This murder case.'

'I'm trying to represent a client,' I said, 'and I'm being

harassed by the police. You have no right to search me.'

The officer said, 'For your information, Lam, someone broke into the residence of Dale Finchley this evening, broke the coroner's seals which had been placed on the doors, and ransacked the place. One of the neighbours tipped off the police and we made an inspection. The person who was in the place drove away at high speed with the police car in pursuit. The police car would have caught up all right but blew a tire.

'The officer fired one warning shot and then shot for a rear tire and then for the gas tank.'

'Nobody's been shooting at me,' I said.

'That's what you say. We find you innocently parked at the curb. You're figuring in this case just too much, my friend.'

The officer searched me but didn't go through my notebook or my billfold. He did, however, find the key to the house at 1369 Hemmet. Fortunately, there was nothing on the key to tell what house it fitted.

'You've got lots of keys,' the officer said.

'I have lots of doors to open.'

'You've got a leather key container full of keys in your right-hand hip pocket; you've got a leather key container with another key in it in your left-hand coat pocket; you've got a single key in your right-hand coat pocket.'

'So what?'

'What doors do they fit?'

I said, 'I have an apartment; I have an office; I have various and sundry transactions for clients. I don't have to tell you the history of every key or what door it fits. If you want to go to the place where Finchley was killed, however, and try my keys on the doors, you're welcome to do so.'

'That,' the officer said, 'is exactly what we're going to do. You follow behind me and keep in touch.'

I followed him to the palatial Finchley residence. The officer patiently tried every key I had on both the front door and back door, then gave it up.

'All right,' he said, 'you can go, but you'll probably be hearing from Sellers about this. Sellers thinks you're figuring in this case altogether too prominently.'

'And you can tell Sellers that I think he's figuring in the case altogether too prominently,' I said.

The officer grinned.

'Well, I'll be on my way,' I told him.

'Just a minute,' the officer said. 'I've got to wait and see if there's a report on you from headquarters. I've put in a request for information.'

'How long do I wait?'

'About ten minutes.'

I knew at that that the officer had telephoned communications to put a tail on me.

I didn't see the shadow report to the officer. Probably it was done by some kind of a radio signal. But after about twelve minutes, the officer said, 'You can go now, Lam; but keep your nose clean.'

I knew they had at least two people shadowing me, so I went to my apartment and stayed there.

There was no place else to go, except to see how Daphne was making out; and if I went down there, I would simply be playing bird dog for the officers.

I knew that Frank Sellers would *very* much like to talk with Daphne Creston.

CHAPTER TWELVE

I STEERED clear of the office the next morning, drove around casually, and located my shadow.

As nearly as I could tell, there was only one shadow. It was a routine job.

I waited until after nine o'clock, then telephoned Orville Maxton.

'Donald Lam talking, Mr. Maxton,' I said.

'What can I do for you?' he asked.

'Give me a little information about the board of the subdivision and improvement commission you are on.'

'Nothing doing. I've talked too much about that already, and I'm not talking any more.'

'I don't want the conventional type of information,' I said. 'I want something different.'

'Such as what?'

'Such as your private opinion of Dale Finchley.'

'Who are you – a reporter?'

'No, I'm a suspect.'

'A what?' he shouted into the telephone.

'A suspect.'

'How come?'

'That's what I'd like to find out,' I said. 'The police are making trouble for me.'

'How well did you know Finchley?'

'Not at all, but I think I'm beginning to find out about him.'

There was a cautious silence at the other end of the line;

then the voice said, 'What did you want to talk to me about?'

'About fifteen minutes,' I said.

'I don't need any wisecracks.'

'That wasn't a wisecrack,' I told him. 'I want to talk with you about fifteen minutes. You don't have to say anything you don't want to; you don't have to answer any questions you don't want to. The police haven't given you a clean bill of health, but they're trying to pin the crime on me. We might have something in common.'

There was silence at the other end of the line; then the voice said, 'I'll give you fifteen minutes. Come on over. How long will it take you to get here?'

'Give me ten minutes and I'll be there.'

'All right, come in ten minutes, and you'll have fifteen – unless I think you're trying to cut corners. And if you are, you'll get thrown out.'

'Fair enough,' I told him.

Actually, Maxton's office was only about two blocks from where I was telephoning. I walked the distance and gave my name to the receptionist in his office.

She looked at me curiously, said, 'Go on in, Mr. Lam. He's expecting you.'

Orville Maxton was a football player type of individual – broad-shouldered, chunky, thick-necked, with heavy brows, a short tough-looking nose, a square jaw, and big hands.

He sized me up with gray eyes which gave the impression of pin-point pupils.

'Sit down, Lam,' he said.

I sat down.

'What do you want to know?'

I said, 'You're a member of a board; you were about to award contracts; Finchley was acting as the board's attorney. Was there any particular reason for Finchley to have all of those bids ready to submit to the board?'

'Sure there was. We were going to award a contract. We wanted to know with whom we were dealing and the amount of the bids.'

'And you had a meeting scheduled?'

Thick, stubby fingers drummed on the desk. 'The meeting was to be called.'

'By whom?'

'By Finchley.'

'When?'

'He said he had one more bid which he thought might be the best of all – that it had been delayed somewhat, but it was coming in ... Look here, Lam; I've told all of this to the police.'

'You didn't tell them where you were at the time of the murder.'

'You're damned right I didn't! It's none of their business! You talk about cooperating with the police; how much cooperation do you *get* from the police?

'They come and ask you all sorts of private questions, and then they call in the newspaper reporters to tell what smart cookies they are – and the first thing you know you read about your private affairs all over the front page of the newspaper!'

'I take it you are referring to your own private affairs?'

'You can take anything you damn please, anywhere you damn please. Now, tell me about yourself.'

I said, 'I'm a private detective.'

'The hell you are!'

'I was working on a case for a woman who had been led into a bigamous marriage. When her husband found out she knew he had another wife living here in Los Angles, he ducked out and cleaned out all of her lifetime savings when he left.

'I managed to trace him to Los Angles. I wanted to put the bite on him.

'I'm keeping my client under cover. For reasons which I can't discuss at the moment, the police feel that she might – just might be the mysterious woman who was in the Finchley house at the time of the murder or the one who was seen leaving the Finchley house shortly after the murder.'

'You act as if you were talking about two women.'

'I think I am.'

Maxton did some more drumming on the top of the desk with his fingertips. His hands were nervous, but his face was steady as a granite cliff.

'What else?' he asked me after a while.

I said, 'The police don't like it when a private detective holds out on them. I'm not in a position to take the police into my confidence at the moment. I'm trying to keep my client under cover. The police are making things hot for me. The best way I can ease the pressure is to find some clue that I can turn over to them and trust to luck they'll go baying off on the scent and leave me alone.'

'So you came to me.'

'I came to you.'

'With the idea that the police are following you and trying to find out what you're up to and that this will start them following *my* trail?'

'With the idea,' I said, 'that I can get some information.'

'Do the police know you're here?'

'I think so. They're having me followed. At least I think they are.'

'I want to keep out of this,' he said. 'I have private reasons for keeping out of it.'

He was the sort of a bull-necked, barrel-chested individual who was strongly vital. He wasn't the type who teams up with one woman and remains true to her for very long at a time.

He looked at me, and I didn't say anything.

'Private, personal reasons,' he said, 'I'm not telling them to the police; I'm not telling them to you; and I don't care to have my private life spread all over the front pages of the metropolitan press.'

'Fair enough,' I told him. 'Now will you answer a question?'

'What?'

'Do you have any reason to believe that, back of his front

of respectability, Dale Finchley was a very shrewd, very clever manipulator?'

He shot a question at me so that the words had almost a physical impact. 'Do you?' he asked.

'Yes,' I said.

He was thoughtfully silent. 'Would you give me your information without getting information from me? In other words, would you just put yourself in my hands and let me play the game my way?'

'No.'

'I didn't think you would.'

I said, 'You wouldn't put your information in my hands and let me play the game the way I want to.'

'No,' he said, 'I wouldn't. But I *could* use a smart private detective.'

I said, 'Suppose copies of all those bids were available to a Johnny-come-lately bidder, who could put in his bid on the job with the assurance that he knew exactly what the other people were bidding. How much would that be worth to that contractor?'

'Anywhere from half a million to a million, provided he had detailed copies of the calls for subcontracts and the specifications for future work prepared by our engineers, together with their estimates – all in all, quite a mass of data.'

I said, 'I think I can show you something if you have an hour to spare.'

'And what do you want in return?'

'If I get in a fight, I'd like to have your influence behind me.'

'I daresay you would. Lots of people would.'

'But I'd leave it up to you to draw your own conclusions.'

'I wouldn't be obligated?'

'Not for a minute.'

He reached for his hat and said, 'How long?'

'About an hour,' I said. 'Now listen,' I told him. 'I'm being shadowed. Probably you're being shadowed. We've got to do some fancy stuff on ditching those shadows.'

'You have any ideas?' he asked.

'Shadowing is my business,' I said. 'I know how to shadow, and that means I know some pretty good gags for getting rid of shadows.'

'I'm willing to be educated.'

'The first thing,' I said, is to act innocent until you get ready to jerk the rug out from under the shadow. Now, you and I are having a friendly conference. You're a tenant here in the building. Presumably you have some influence. You ring up the janitor of the building and tell him you want him to bring up a freight elevator and hold it at the seventh floor. We're on the ninth floor.

'We go to the elevator,' I said. 'Shadows are probably watching the entrance, and another shadow may be up here somewhere in the corridor. This is the ninth floor. We get in the elevator; we drop down two floors to the seventh floor; we hurry to the freight elevator; the janitor takes us down to the basement; we go out in the alley. We go down the alley until we find an unlocked back door of a store building; we go in that door; we come out the front; we pick up a taxicab; we go to a drive-yourself place and rent a car.'

'That seems like a lot of trouble to get rid of shadows.'

'It takes a lot of trouble to get rid of a good shadow.'

'You think they'll fall for it?'

'The man on the ninth floor,' I said. 'will expect the shadow in the lobby of the building to pick us up when we go out. If we act as though we didn't know we were being shadowed, we can probably get by with it.'

Maxton picked up the telephone, said to his secretary, 'Get me the manager of the building.' Then after a moment he said, 'This is Orville Maxton. I want the janitor to take a freight elevator up to the seventh floor. That's right, a freight elevator. That's right, the seventh floor. I want him to wait there until we come. I'll give him two minutes to get into position.'

He listened for a moment, grinned, said, 'Thank you,' then hung up.

We waited about two minutes. The phone rang. Maxton answered it, said to me, 'The freight elevator is in position.'

'Let's go,' I told him.

We sauntered out of his office together, down the corridor and into the elevator.

A man who had been standing at the water fountain walked casually into a real-estate office.

The elevator door closed. Maxton said, 'Out at seven, please.'

We got out at the seventh floor. Maxton led the way down the deserted corridor to a freight elevator.

A Swedish janitor asked apprehensively, 'What's the trouble? Something missing? Something I did wrong?'

'No trouble, Ole,' Maxton said, and handed him five dollars. 'Let's go down all the way to the alley entrance.'

'Yah,' Ole said, and the freight elevator rumbled down.

Maxton looked at me and grinned. 'You know, Lam,' he said, 'I'm beginning to like you. I think you know your job.'

'Thanks,' I told him.

We got out in the alley, found the back door of a sporting-goods store that was open, went in, walked through the store talking to each other as though completely engrossed in conversation, walked past a couple of clerks who wanted to sell us something but didn't want to interrupt, went out on the sidewalk, got a taxi-cab, went to a drive-yourself agency, picked up a car, and drove to 1369 Hemmet.

I parked the car, took the key from my pocket and unlocked the door.

'What kind of a setup *is* this?' Maxton asked.

'That,' I said, 'is something you can tell me.'

I went into the dining room.

There wasn't as much as a trace of furniture in the place.

'Well?' Maxton asked.

I turned and led the way out. 'Come on,' I told him.

'What's the idea of coming out here?'

'I wanted to show you something.'

'Well, show it to me.'

'It's gone.'

'Where?'

'That,' I said, 'is something I'd like to find out.'

'Can you tell me what it was?'

'Furniture of a sort.'

'What kind of furniture?'

'A battery of five duplicating machines,' I said. 'The latest electronic duplicators.'

He looked at me and blinked thoughtfully, then said after a moment, 'I don't get it.'

I said, 'You've been in Finchley's residence from time to time.'

'Certainly. He did a lot of business from his residence, and I've done a lot of business with Finchley.'

I said, 'How far is Finchley's place from here?'

He looked thoughtful, then said, 'Why, it's only a matter of four blocks.'

I didn't say anything more but led the way out of the house, our footsteps echoing loudly across the deserted living room and the reception corridor.

I locked the door behind us, went over to the adjoining house on the east.

'Can you tell me,' I asked, 'what time the moving van came to the house next door?'

'I certainly can,' the woman who answered the door said indignantly. 'It was two-thirty this morning.'

'You didn't happen to notice the name on the moving van, did you?'

'I did not. I don't get up and try to notice things at two-thirty in the morning. I tried to get back to sleep.'

'Were they noisy?'

'They never said a word, but that big van lumbered up there and stopped and men got out and went in and came out carrying things. And the house is supposed to be empty. And I'll tell you this much: they had blankets of some sort over the side of the van so you couldn't read any names.'

'At two-thirty this morning?'

'Yes. Now, tell me, why do you want to know?'

I said, 'I'm thinking of buying the place and I wanted to be sure that everything was out of it.'

'Well, everything was supposed to be out of it, but they certainly took a truckload of stuff. Not one of those great big vans, but a covered van just the same.'

'Thank you very much indeed,' I told her.

I turned to Maxton. 'All right,' I said. 'We go back to the office of the rental agency, turn the car in, and take a cab back to your office building. We go in the alley entrance, and your Swede janitor takes us up in the freight elevator. With luck, the shadows will never know we went out.'

Maxton said, 'Lam, I'm beginning to put this stuff together.'

'That's fine.'

'You've told me something that is beginning to ring a bell – some very, very valuable information.'

'I was hoping you could use it.'

'I can use it, but I don't know just how.'

We went through our routine and took the elevator up to the ninth floor.

The man who had been loitering around the drinking fountain and who had entered the real-estate office was no longer visible as we came in.

'Where's your car?' Maxton asked.

'Down in a parking lot a couple of blocks from here. I walked.'

'And you think you were tailed?' Maxton asked.

'I don't think there's any doubt about it.'

Maxton said, 'Where can I get hold of you if I need you, Lam?'

I gave him one of my cards.

He looked at me thoughtfully for a moment, said, 'You may be a hell of a sight smarter than you look.' And then he added after a moment, 'and you don't look exactly dumb.'

He grinned. For the first time since I had met him, I got a good look at his teeth.

His big hand squeezed on mine. 'Thanks a lot, Lam,' he said. 'I think maybe things are going to work out all right. You and I are in the same boat. I've got to turn up a new clue sooner or later in order to keep the police from making a big issue out of where I was at the time the murder was committed.'

'You know where you were?'

'Of course I know where I was! And only one other person knows, and I'm not particularly anxious to have the identity of that other person disclosed to the reading public.'

'O.K.,' I told him. 'You can reach me if you need me.'

I went back to the elevator, slipped the operator five bucks and said, 'Basement.'

The cage took me down to the basement. I grinned at Ole, waved him a friendly greeting, and calmly walked out the back door as though Maxton had fixed it all up for me.

I went back to the drive-yourself agency, rented another car, went out and made enough crazy turns to make certain I wasn't being followed, then went to the apartment where I'd left Daphne Creston.

Some sixth sense warned me something was wrong when I gently fitted the key to the door.

I opened it a crack. 'Everybody decent?' I asked.

There was no answer. I stepped inside.

The place looked as though it had been struck by a cyclone. The bedcovers had been pulled off the bed and were on the floor. The mattress had been jerked off and was standing in a corner. Drawers had been pulled out of the bureau, clothes taken from the closet and tossed on the floor.

I heard the sound of motion coming from the kitchenette, then the clatter of pans.

I jerked open the door.

Katherine Elliott was there in the kitchen in front of a cupboard, jerking out pots and pans, then searching the corners with a flashlight.

I stood there in the doorway.

After a moment she looked up, saw me, stifled a scream, then straightened.

'Hello, Katherine,' I said.

'You!' she said, and her face really showed startled surprise.

'Who did you expect?'

'How did you find me here?'

I grinned at her and said, 'I followed you.'

'No, you didn't. Nobody could have followed me.'

'You don't know a good shadowing job when you see one,' I told her. 'Find what you're looking for?'

'You,' she told me, 'can go to hell! And I may be able to help send you there. You're a murderer!'

'And,' I told her, 'you're alone with me!'

Suddenly the idea dawned on her. She let the panic show on her face.

I moved toward her.

She flattened herself against the wall, eased toward the back door, suddenly went out and down the service steps.

I made a bolt for the front door – not bothering even to close the door behind me. I couldn't wait for the slow, rattling elevator. I took the steps two at a time, got out on the sidewalk and started checking the automobiles that were parked in front of the place.

The third had a registration slip showing that it was the property of Katherine Elliott.

I stood close to the car, drew my .38-caliber revolver and put two bullet holes through the body of the car – one of them just above the gas tank in the rear, the other one along the side of the car, where it left an unsightly gash by the back door.

I shoved the revolver in my holster and made a run to my rented car, jumped in and drove off just as some curious pedestrian – hearing the sounds of the shots – started looking around, wondering whether they were shots or whether a truck had backfired.

CHAPTER THIRTEEN

I DROVE directly to the office, parked the car, walked into Bertha's office and said, 'O.K. Bertha, we're having a show-down!'

'How come?'

'Come on,' I told her; 'we're going to call on Katherine Elliott. We go to her apartment. She's going to try to beat us to the punch. We can't afford to have her do it.'

'So what do we do?'

'We search her apartment.'

'Without a warrant?'

'Without a warrant. She's been searching my place. We'll return the compliment.'

'And how do we get in?'

I said, 'we're going to have Frank Sellers with us. Call him on the phone.'

Bertha sighed. 'Do you know what you're doing Donald?'

'I know I'm doing the only thing possible under the circumstances.'

Bertha picked up the telephone, called police headquarters, asked for Frank Sellers, and got him on the phone.

'Frank,' she said, 'this is Bertha Cool. Donald is having a brainstorm.'

There were squawks at the other end of the line.

'All right,' Bertha said, 'I've got him with me. We want to meet with you.'

Bertha Cool held the phone turned to me and said, 'You've

been cutting corners. Sellers is going to take you into custody for interrogation.'

'Let him interrogate,' I said. 'But tell him to meet us at the Steelbuilt Apartments. That's his only chance of getting in touch with me. Tell him I'll be watching the entrance to the apartments and, when he drives up I'll contact him.'

Bertha relayed the message to Sellers.

Sellers made more squawking noises on the phone.

'Now hang up, Bertha,' I told her. 'Act as if the connection had been broken; and when he calls back, have the office operator tell him that you and I have left the office.'

Bertha hesitated for a moment, then hung up the phone.

'You *don't* do this to a cop!' she said.

'Maybe *you* don't,' I said, 'but I do. Come on, let's go.'

'Just what are you going to do, Donald?'

'You and I together,' I said, 'are going to pull a chestnut out of the fire for Sellers.'

'Will he like it?'

'He'll love it!'

'Well, let's hope so,' she said, 'because he was as mad as a wet cat over the telephone. He says you've been cutting corners again; that he tried to stick up for us and told you to keep your nose clean, but that you weren't content with that. You went trying to take short cuts. You've been ditching shadows.'

'We'll talk on the way,' I told her.

I drove Bertha to the Steelbuilt Apartments in the rented car. We parked by a fire hydrant.

Sellers came up in a police car in about two minutes. Sellers was mad.

'Bertha,' he said, 'I've tried to protect you through all of this, but this time that little bastard has gone too far!'

'Perhaps not far enough,' I told him.

'Well,' he said, 'if overshooting the mark is far enough, you've really done it.'

I said, 'One of your men was shooting at a car last night.'

'Was he?'

'A car down by the Finchley residence.'

Sellers' eyes narrowed. 'Know anything about it?' he asked.

'Stick around here,' I said, 'and you'll find a car with two bullet holes in it driving up here in about the next ten minutes.'

Sellers surveyed me with blinking eyes; then he said thoughtfully, 'If you've got a car with bullet holes in it, Pint Size, you've got something! Whose is it?'

'It's the property of Katherine Elliott, who lives in apartment 14 B.'

Sellers was thoughtful. 'If she has a car with two bullet holes in it,' he said, 'I would be justified in getting a search warrant.'

'And what good would that do you?'

'I don't know, but we could at least look.'

'And by that time, everything would be gone.'

'What makes you think it would be gone?'

'She knows the fat is in the fire.'

'How does she know it?'

'Because she's got two bullet holes in her car.'

'Now, wait a minute – wait a minute,' Sellers said. 'If this is some of your shenanigans, I want to know about it. I want to be able to evaluate the evidence ... Well, if I've got to get a search warrant, I want to be acting in good faith.'

I said, 'By the time you get a search warrant, Katherine will be gone and the evidence will be gone. If you're going to do anything, you've got to get up to that apartment within ten seconds after Katherine Elliott gets there.'

'I can't search without a warrant. Do you think she'd give me permission?'

'She wouldn't give you the time of day,' I said. 'But if you had reason, as a police officer, to go into the apartment and then you uncovered evidence ...'

'What kind of evidence?'

'Wait and see.'

'But how would I have reason to go in there as a peace officer?'

'That,' I said, 'is the nice part of the Supreme Court decisions. As a police officer, your wrists are handcuffed behind your back; you can't do anything with a suspected criminal without giving him a warning, telling him he's entitled to be represented by an attorney, warning that he doesn't need to answer any questions. In other words if you kick your case out of the window, you can talk with the suspect; if you talk with the suspect without kicking your case out of the window, you don't get anywhere.'

'You don't need to tell me anything about the Supreme Court decisions!' Sellers said bitterly.

'You'll learn to live with them,' I told him.

'I'm going to have to,' he said. 'But I'm not going to like it.'

'But,' I told him, 'the Supreme Court has left one beautiful loophole. If some private detective violates the rights of the prisoner all to hell and then you enter the picture and if the evidence of guilt is lying all around, the Supreme Court can't tell you to close your eyes.'

'And how do we get a situation of that sort?' he asked.

I jerked my thumb toward Bertha.

Sellers said, 'Dammit it, Donald, you and your schemes and ...'

'Shut up!' I said. 'Here she comes!'

I pushed Sellers back behind the automobile.

Katherine Elliott was too disturbed to pay any attention to anything. She slammed her car into a parking place, banged the bumper of the car behind her, shut off the motor, jerked the key out of the car, and ran into the entrance to the apartment house.

'Come on,' I told Sellers. 'We haven't got all day, you know.'

We headed across the street – Bertha waddling to keep up with us.

He paused long enough to study the bullet holes; then we headed for the apartment house entrance.

Bertha said, 'What do you want me to do, Donald?'

'Do your stuff, Bertha,' I told her.

'Rough?' she asked.

'The rougher the better.'

'Can we get by with it?'

'Yes.'

'Donald,' she sighed, 'you're a brainy little bastard! I've played ball with you before and, so help me, I'll do it again!'

We walked into the lobby of the apartment house. Sellers showed his ID card to the man at the desk, and we went up in the elevator.

I knocked on the door of 14B.

For a moment there was no answer.

I knocked again and said, 'Police officer checking your car, madam. You have bullet holes in it.'

The door opened a cautious crack. Katherine Elliott said, 'I want to report that to the police. A private detective, Donald Lam, deliberately shot those holes in my car and...'

She broke off as Bertha Cool pushed the door open and said, 'Mind if we come in, dearie?'

Bertha led the way into the apartment.

Katherine Elliott, said, 'You're damn right I mind.' And then, seeing me, she pointed a finger at me and said, '*There's* the man that put the bullet holes in my car.'

Sellers looked at me, and I saw the idea crash home into his consciousness. Sellers knew she was telling the truth and he wanted out.

'You'll make a complaint, madam?' he asked.

'I'll make a complaint,' she said.

Sellers said, 'You understand that's a serious offense – or rather, a series of offenses. It involves malicious destruction of property, discharging a firearm within the city limits. If you make a complaint, I don't want you to back out on me.'

'I'm making a complaint,' she said.

'Where did this happen?' I asked.

'*You* know where it happened. My car was parked in front of ...'

'Yes, yes. Go on,' I said, as her voice trailed into silence.

'I don't have to answer *your* questions,' she blazed, and then turned to Sellers. 'Officer, I want action! I want this man taken into custody. He's been trying to make trouble for me in every conceivable way. He's been to the Better Business Bureau and complained about me. He's tried to annoy and harass me, all because I have some information that he wants and won't give it to him.'

Sellers said, 'I told you you'd get into trouble one of these days, Pint Size. *Did* you put those bullet holes in that car?'

I looked at him and laughed.

'Be your age,' I said. 'The police were chasing a car last night and fired a couple of shots. You find her car with a couple of bullet holes in it. Why don't you ask her *where* she was last night and what she was doing out on Hemmet Avenue?'

Sellers looked back at her and, at what he saw in her face, did a sudden double-take. A lot of the assurance that he'd had began to evaporate.

I said, 'Look around, Bertha.'

Bertha barged through the apartment.

'Don't you dare search my apartment!' Katherine Elliott screamed. 'Don't you dare! I'll ... Officer, protect me!'

'You can't search the apartment, Bertha,' Sellers warned.

Bertha paid no attention either to him or to Katherine Eliott but kept on toward the kitchenette. She pushed open a folding door, looked around, turned back. And Katherine Elliott was on her like a wildcat, clawing, screaming obscenities, and trying to get a handful of Bertha's hair.

Bertha scooped an arm around the woman's waist, picked her up off the floor and slammed her on the bed so hard the pictures rattled against the wall.

Sellers started to move toward Bertha, then thought better about it.

Bertha moved majestically toward a closed door, opened the door to disclose a bathroom.

A gurgling, inarticulate sound came from the room.

Bertha stepped inside.

'Fry me for an oyster,' she said.

I reached Bertha's side in a few quick strides while Sellers was still standing rooted to the floor and Katherine Elliott was trying to get her breath back.

Daphne Creston had been wrapped in a bed sheet; then the bed sheet had been tied around her so it made a strait jacket. She had been gagged and put in the bath-tub. She was lying there helpless, only her panic-stricken eyes pleading for help.

Bertha took one look, then whirled away from the door.

'Take a look in here, Sergeant,' I said.

Katherine Elliott came up off the bed like a trampoline performer clearing the net. She just doubled her back and raised her feet, used her hands for propulsion and shot off the bed, her skirts almost to her shoulders.

When she hit the floor, she was headed for the door.

Bertha was incredibly fast for a short, heavy woman who had to waddle. She was like an army tank crossing the room.

Katherine had a hand on the door and the door half open when Bertha grabbed the back of her hair.

'Oh, no, you don't, dearie,' Bertha said, and jerked. Katherine screamed.

Bertha looped an arm around Katherine's waist, slammed her back on the bed.

I was bending over the bathtub fumbling with the knots.

The first one I untied was the one which held the gag in place. I pulled the bandage off her mouth, pulled the gag out of the mouth with my fingers.

Daphne made spitting noises, then said, 'Donald – oh, Donald – I knew you'd come.'

Sellers said, 'What the hell is *this* all about?'

I said to Bertha, 'Watch her, Bertha.'

Bertha said, 'I'm watching her. You stay there, dearie, or I'll sit on your stomach and hold you in place.'

I tried my hand at the knots on the torn sheet.

Sellers said, 'Let me cut it Donald. We may need those knots for evidence. Do you know what the hell this is all about?'

'Yes.'

'Well, you'd better tell me.'

I got the bonds cut and the sheet ripped off Daphne. Her skirts were pretty well up, and I started to pull them down.

'To hell with the legs,' Daphne said. 'Get me out of this porcelain mausoleum.'

Sellers and I lifted her out.

Daphne tried to stand up. The circulation had pretty well gone in her legs. She stumbled and would have fallen if I hadn't caught her. She lurched against me, her head on my shoulder.

'My legs are full of pins and needles,' she said.

'How long have you been there?' I asked.

'I don't know. I guess an hour and a half anyway.'

'Did you get my Special Delivery letter?' I asked.

She nodded.

'Then what did you do?'

'I was independent, Donald. I couldn't sponge on you any more. I didn't want to leave the brief case in the apartment, so I put it in a safe place. It's . . .'

'Never mind for the moment, Daphne,' I said. 'It's in a safe place. What did you do next?'

'I took the three hundred dollars and was careful to clean up the apartment. I was sure I didn't leave any ring in the bathtub and had things so they would be nice for you. I was just leaving when Katherine Elliott drove up and said, "Mr. Harper has decided he wants you after all. I have the three hundred dollars for you in my office. If you'll just come with me and sign the receipt, I'll notify Mr. Harper."

'I started to tell her that I already had the three hundred

dollars; and then I knew what had happened – that you had dug down in your pocket and had put up three hundred dollars for me. . . . Well, like a ninny I just came along with her. We went up to this apartment and Miss Elliott said that Harper was due here at any minute but we'd have a cup of coffee.

'I know now that she drugged that coffee. I drank it and began to feel dizzy. I told her I thought I was going to faint. She helped me into the bathroom and then everything started going around and around, and that's the last I remember until I found myself all tied up and gagged the way you found me. I tried to scream and couldn't. I tried to kick my heels against the bathtub but I couldn't do any good.

'She'd taken my shoes off. I had a deathly fear that somehow somebody was going to turn on the water and I'd drown in there like a trapped rat. Donald, you've no idea what I've been through!'

Sellers said, 'Will you kindly tell me what this is all about, Pint Size?'

I said, 'Katherine Elliott is a girl who plays both ends against the middle. She's been in trouble with the Better Business Bureau over things she's done. She has a collection of hole-in-the-wall offices that she rents out by the hour, by the day, or by the week and gives an air of respectability and a telephone number to anyone who wants to pull a fly-by-night deal.

'Dale Finchley was a political lawyer. He also knew which side of the bread had the butter. He'd been playing ball with Lathrop, Lucas and Manly, subdivision contractors.

'It was a slick scheme. He'd let the contractors who had the inside track copy all of the bids and then sneak in their own bid at the last minute. They could be just a thousand or two under the lowest bid and be assured of getting the job.

'Naturally that cost money.

'This man Harper she talks about in reality is Walter Lucas.

'The night Finchley was murdered, Lucas was to go there and pick up all the bids, then rush them to a vacant house four blocks away where he had a whole set of duplicating machines set up. They would duplicate the bids, then restore the originals, telephone that they were making a bid of a couple of thousand dollars lower than the lowest bid but that they needed a few hours to get it in in detail.

'They'd work all night pirating the specific information they wanted from the other bids and show up bright and early in the morning with a bona fide bid that would enable them to be sure they got the job.

'But a few days before the deal was to be pulled off, Katherine Elliott reported that there were suspicious circumstances, that someone had been questioning her in her office.

'Actually Katherine here was preparing to put the bite on everybody. She had been getting all the deadwood on Finchley, and she'd been working with Lucas.

'I doubt if the other partners knew what was going on. I think it will turn out that Walter Lucas was the only really crooked one in the outfit, but Lucas had charge of the bids on this type of construction, and Lucas and Finchley were carrying on a slick scheme of double cross; then somebody found out about it and started blackmailing Lucas, and Lucas would have given his right arm to find out who the blackmailer was. All he knew for certain was that someone was putting the bite on him and he was being forced to leave money in various places, after receiving mysterious telephone calls disclosing information which he thought no one else had.

'It never occurred to him that it could be Katherine Elliott. He thought she was a rather dumb accomplice who was renting him offices from time to time under an assumed name.

'But with this big deal coming up, Lucas had a tip that someone was going to try to make trouble. Lucas wanted copies of the papers, but he didn't want trouble. He had everything all fixed up with Finchley. What he needed was a patsy who could act as the go-between, someone whose veracity could be impeached, someone who would tell a story that was incredible on the face of it if picked up for questioning. If things went smoothly, Lucas would wind up with copies of all the bids and all the confidential engineering estimates. If things didn't go right, Lucas would be in a position to call the patsy an unmitigated liar if the finger of suspicion ever pointed at him. So Lucas put an ad in the paper which would be designed to attract a patsy of the type he was looking for.

'The ad looked all right on the face of it, but what it really said was "WANTED: Someone who is down on his luck, who is willing to commit perjury for three hundred dollars." '

'You can prove all this?' Sellers asked.

I grinned at him. '*You* can,' I said, 'as soon as you get the lead out and start your investigation.'

'Who killed Finchley?' he asked.

'Use your judgment,' I said. 'A woman was in there. Finchley accused her of being a traitor – a woman who wanted to make one last stake with blackmail and then get out of the country.'

'You lie! You lie!' Katherine Elliott screamed. 'I was never near the place!'

'That sounds reasonable,' I said, 'with two bullet holes in your car.'

'*You* put those bullet holes there!'

'Talk to the police about it,' I said. 'They're looking for a car with bullet holes in it.'

'What about this young woman?'

Sellers jerked his head toward Daphne Creston.

'This woman,' I said, 'is Daphne Creston. They picked her as a patsy. She's your star witness. She was in the house and heard Finchley accuse Katherine Elliott of double-crossing him and being a traitor. Katherine thought he'd be an easy mark for blackmail; but Finchley, after deciding to play ball, changed his mind. He told her she couldn't get a nickel out of him. He started to call the police.

'Katherine was furious, and she couldn't afford to be unmasked as the blackmailer who was putting the bite on Walter Lucas. She lost her head, shot Finchley, and dashed out the back door.

'She probably had her car parked in the alley. Anyhow, she managed to make a clean getaway. But she knew that Finchley had left plans in a brief case to be turned over to Walter Lucas, and she suspected there was another brief case with blackmail money in it.

'Katherine decided either I or Daphne probably had a brief case with a wad of dough in it. I'd given her the address of my dummy apartment when I'd answered the ad. She went there and found Daphne.

'Katherine Elliott lured Daphne out of the apartment, then went back with her keys – and you should see that apartment now. You'd think it had been in the eye of a cyclone.'

The thought of the wrecked apartment was devastating to Daphne's pride as a housekeeper. 'Oh, Donald,' she said. 'I left it *so* neat!'

Sellers seemed halfway undecided. 'Dammit, Donald,' he said, 'you always get me into these things! Tell me one thing: did you put the bullet holes in that car?'

'You're asking me?' I said.

'Yes.'

'You're entirely out of order, Sergeant. The minute a crime passes the investigative phase and gets to the point where you're accusing anyone of a crime, you have to go through a long rigmarole; and you can't question a suspect except in the presence of a lawyer. You should know that.'

Sellers stood undecided, feet planted wide apart. Slowly, automatically he reached in his pocket, fished out a cigar and pushed it in his mouth. 'It's a hell of a story!' he said.

'The newspapers will love it,' I told him. 'They'll want some pictures of you.'

'How the hell can I prove all this?' Sellers asked.

I started looking around.

'The gun that fired the bullet that killed Finchley should be around here somewhere. Here's the amateur's favourite hiding place,' I said, and I noticed there were some little gritty grains on the kitchen floor.

I opened a cupboard door, picked out a big tin can marked 'Sugar'. I upended the can over the sink.

Sugar cascaded out, and then a snub-nosed, blue-steel .38 Colt revolver.

'There's your murder case, Sergeant,' I said.

Katherine Elliott screamed, 'Walter Lucas is a crook. He's going to turn against me and try to blame everything on me. He's mixed in it deeper than I am.'

Sellers shifted the wet cigar in his mouth and said, 'Come on, Sister; you're going to take a ride to headquarters. You're entitled to a lawyer. You don't have to say anything.'

CHAPTER FOURTEEN

'What did you do with the money, Daphne?' I asked when Sellers had taken Katherine Elliott to headquarters.

'It was in my purse. She took it.'

'No, no – not the three hundred – the forty thousand.'

She said, 'When I was getting ready to leave the apartment, I didn't want to leave it there, and I didn't know *what* to do, so I took it down to the station, put it in one of the lockers, took the key to the locker, put it in an envelope and mailed it to you at your office, Special Delivery. It should be there by this time.'

'We'll just keep that as an ace in the hole,' I said. 'Come on. We're going to the office.'

'All three of us,' Bertha said.

Barney Adams was sitting in Bertha Cool's private office when we got there. He looked from Bertha Cool to me. He slowly shook his head.

'A friend at headquarters has just tipped me off,' he said. 'How the hell you did it is more than I know.'

'But we did it,' Bertha said.

'You did it,' Adams admitted.

'What's all this hooey about your Continental Divide Insurance and Indemnity?' Bertha asked.

'I'm sorry,' Adams said. 'Actually, I represent the League of Civic Supervision.

'We had a tip that there was some crooked work going on in bidding and that Katherine Elliott was the go-between. While we were trying to investigate, we saw this ad in the paper and decided to start our investigation there.

'I felt certain that any good private detective would see an opportunity to be selected as the patsy and would, apparently, fall for the three hundred-dollar bait in order to find out what it was all about.

'I had cultivated Katherine Elliott by letting her think that I was a fly-by-night broker who wanted to rent some of her offices, and I'd established a pretty good contact there. We became friendly.

'Through her I found out that Donald Lam had appeared and had been turned down. Naturally I was somewhat bitter. I thought that Donald should have done better than that. I thought he would either have had someone who was less sophisticated play the patsy or that he would have been able to appear as more of a rural character.'

'Donald would have done all right,' Bertha said, 'if it hadn't been for this Daphne Creston showing up. She was made to order for what they wanted.'

'Yes,' Adams said, 'that's where I jumped at a wrong conclusion. I decided that Donald had appeared too sophisticated for the job and had been turned down. I was trying to find out the real identity of Rodney Harper. It never occurred to me he was connected with a big contracting firm or that Finchley was letting a competitor have an inside track on the bids. We did know that Lathrop, Lucas and Manly had been getting more than their fair share of contracts, that their bids had been just a few dollars under the lowest bidder; and we thought there *might* be something wrong, but we couldn't put our finger on it.'

'Well, you've got your finger on it now,' Bertha told him.

'I'll say,' Adams admitted.

'Next time,' I told him, 'you'd do a lot better not to mix into the case yourself. I laid a trap for Katherine Elliott, and who should walk into it but you.'

'You mean that lunch engagement?'

'I mean that lunch engagement,' I said.

'It wasn't lunch. I just met her for cocktails, and then I looked around and found that just by chance your secretary was having a pre-lunch cocktail in the bar. She hadn't seen me yet, and I didn't want her to see me, so I told Katherine I'd get in touch with her later on, to wait two or three minutes, pay the check and go back to her office.

'Then I ducked into the men's room and waited there for nearly half an hour before I came out. When I came out your secretary had finished her cocktail and was gone.'

I said, 'I was laying a trap for Katherine Elliott. I wanted her to lead me to someone. She put through a telephone call and evidently spilled what she had to say over the telephone, which was to the effect that I wasn't a prospective patsy at all but was getting very, very close to things they wanted to keep under cover. And then you had to come blundering along and walk into the trap.'

'I really owe you an apology for that,' Adams admitted.

'Apology, hell!' Bertha said. 'We don't want you to owe us an apology. Get out your checkbook!'

Adams heaved a sigh. 'You are,' he said, 'living up to your reputations – both of you.' But he opened his brief case and took out his checkbook.

››› If you've enjoyed this book and would like to discover more great vintage crime and thriller titles, as well as the most exciting crime and thriller authors writing today, visit: ›››

The Murder Room
Where Criminal Minds Meet

themurderroom.com

www.ingramcontent.com/pod-product-compliance
Ingram Content Group UK Ltd.
Pitfield, Milton Keynes, MK11 3LW, UK
UKHW022309280225
455674UK00004B/230

9 781471 909269